THE "LADY" WAS COVERED

"This whore tried to lift my billfold." Both men grabbed for her, and one managed to hook his curled fingers over the top of the chemise at the back. The old and worn fabric of her underwear parted with a vicious ripping sound. Clover was suddenly naked as she streaked away from the hotel.

Suddenly she turned and lunged toward Steele. He was holding out his coat at arm's length toward her. She skidded to a halt, snatched the coat and draped it around her shoulders. This put Steele between herself and the men.

"Step aside, mister," the leader of the bunch said. Jake stepped forward and went for his gun, but the muzzle was not clear of the holster before he was covered. Steele had been holding the rifle ready ever since the whore had run toward him. Almost faster than the eye could see, his left hand came up and across his body. At the same time, he flicked the wrist of his right hand and turned his body slightly from the waist. His thumb cocked the hammer, and his finger took first pressure against the trigger.

"Jesus!" Jake gasped.

Clover looked at Steele. "Never figured I'd have to say thanks to a guy like you," she said grudgingly. "But thanks."

The Virginian showed a quiet smile. "And I never thought I'd give a whore the coat off my back," he answered.

The Steele Series:

#1 REBELS & ASSASSINS DIE HARD
#2 THE BOUNTY HUNTER
#3 HELL'S JUNCTION
#4 VALLEY OF BLOOD
#5 GUN RUN
#6 THE KILLING ART

George G. Gilman

ADAM STEELE

The Killing Art
No. 6

PINNACLE BOOKS   NEW YORK CITY

This is a work of fiction. All the characters and events portrayed in this book are fictional, and any resemblance to real people or incidents is purely coincidental.

STEELE #6: THE KILLING ART

Copyright © 1975 by George G. Gilman

A Pinnacle Books edition, published by special arrangement with New English Library, Limited, London

ISBN: 0-523-00965-8

First printing, December 1976

Cover illustration by Bruce Minney

Printed in the United States of America

PINNACLE BOOKS, INC.
275 Madison Avenue
New York, N. Y. 10016

For ALAN
wherever he may be

The Killing Art

Chapter One

Adam Steele stepped out of Craddock's Barber's Shop on to the main street of Friday Wells and immediately began to sweat. It was only nine-thirty but the morning sun was already extending a threat to fry the eyeballs of anyone crazy enough to look up at it.

"Happy July the Fourth to you, son," a man croaked. "Spare a dime for a feller to celebrate?"

The old-timer was sitting on the edge of the sidewalk, in the dark patch of shade from the barber's shop canopy. From the look of him he had started his Independence Day celebrations early. His hollow-cheeked face was pale through the grime and bristles and his watery eyes were bloodshot above discolored bags. His hand shook badly as he extended it toward Steele.

"Be happy to, if I had a dime," Steele told him, his quiet voice accented with a Virginia drawl.

The drunk's nervous grin became a bitter grimace. His voice took on a whine. "Dude like you

1

just gotta have a king-size bankroll!" He spat between his own feet and then returned his scornful attention to Steele. "I seen you, mister. I knew you was rich. Now I know you're a tightwad to boot."

"Will give you something, feller," the Virginian offered evenly. The drunk showed his rotten teeth in the grin again and splayed his shaking hand. "Piece of advice. Never judge by appearances."

He turned to move along the street and the drunk spat some more contempt.

"And I'll give you some more advice, Joe," Ed Craddock said as he stepped into the open doorway of his shop. "Don't rile that there guy."

Joe used the back of a hand to wipe a dribble of saliva from the corner of his mouth. "Advice don't do nothing to help a man's thirst," he croaked.

Craddock continued to watch the slow-moving, easy gait of Steele. "But if it's took, it could keep a man from gettin' killed," he replied reflectively.

The drunk's error in assuming Steele had a bankroll was understandable. The barber's contention that he was a killer showed that the man was a fine judge of character. As he angled across the dusty street, heading for the entrance of the San Juan Hotel, Steele was considering his chance of making a small bankroll by using one of his killing skills. A two-hundred-and-fifty dollar stake: not to give substance to his rich-looking appearance, but simply to ensure that he and his horse could continue to eat. For the haircut, shave and hot towels had taken his last dollar.

2

"Draw your picture, mister? Only twenty cents."

This time it was a youngster who addressed Steele as the Virginian stepped up on to the sidewalk in front of the hotel. A boy of about eighteen who sat on a small folding chair between two easels. Propped on one of the easels was a thick pad of stiff paper. On the other was a board with a paper sign tacked to it. Around the edges of the sign were charcoal sketches of every president from Washington to Grant. In the center, elegantly lettered, was the legend: BILLY CORNFORD—FAST ON THE DRAW.

"I know what I look like, feller," Steele said as he went on into the hotel, noting little about the artist except that his right shirt sleeve was empty and tucked into the waistband of his pants.

"Send it back home to your folks!" Cornford called after him, but drew no response.

There were already some whores in the lobby, sitting with forced primness on the overstuffed sofas. They looked expectantly at the doorway as Steele entered, then relaxed as they recognized him. The thin-faced desk clerk wore an apologetic look as he handed Steele the key to room ten.

"You won't overlook the matter of the room, sir," he said nervously. Like the barber, he had also spotted something to fear behind the non-chalant facade of the Virginian.

"I'll be out by noon, feller," Steele assured, accepting the key and starting up the carpeted stairway.

"And I for one will be glad to see the back of you!" the redheaded whore with the fake beauty spot on her cheek called after him.

3

"Clover!" the desk clerk snapped anxiously.

"Go to hell!" the redhead retorted.

"He sure won't!" one of the blonde whores rasped, jerking a thumb toward Steele. "Don't smoke, don't drink and don't go with women. Damn angel already is what he is!"

"Yeah!" Clover taunted with a harsh laugh. "Bet he's got wings folded under them fancy threads!"

The desk clerk clapped his hands and glanced up fearfully as Steele reached the second floor balcony and turned to survey the whores in the lobby. "Ladies!" he shouted with shrill anger. "There is no obligation for gentlemen guests of the San Juan Hotel to—"

"He ain't no kinda man!" Clover cut in, her tone a snarl. "Winged angel is what he is!"

The clerk's small eyes became imploring as he watched Steele respond to the taunts with complete indifference. "I apologize on their behalf, sir," he called. "I don't know what's got into them."

"I didn't," Steele answered, swinging around and crossing the balcony to key open the door to his room.

He closed it against a barrage of insults rising above the protests of the clerk. But the noise didn't last for long. It was too hot today to do anything for which there would be no reward. The window of the spartanly furnished, reasonably clean room was open. There was no breeze but Steele dragged the hard seated, straight backed chair away from the wall and placed it in front of the window. He angled it slightly so that when he sat down he would be facing northwest—

4

to the left of where the climbing sun glared yellow and angry out of the cobalt sky. Before he sat down, he rested his rifle against the window sill and took off his jacket to drape it carefully across the rumpled blankets of the unmade bed.

The rifle was old. A six-shot, Colt Hartford revolving model of .44 caliber, Old, but well-cared-for, with a small gold plate screwed to the fire-scorched rosewood stock. On this plate was the inscription: *To Benjamin P. Steele, with gratitude—Abraham Lincoln.*

The jacket on the bed was brand-new. A match for the pants worn by Ben Steele's son. His black boots were new. So was his wide-brim, low-crown gray hat with the black band. His vest—a deeper shade of blue than the suit—and the white shirt with the fancy collar were also less than twenty-four hours out of the Harding Clothing Emporium. The sole detractory item against Steele's dudish appearance was the sweat-stiffened gray kerchief draped around his neck.

The man himself was neither old like the rifle nor new like most of his clothes. He was in his twenty-ninth year and now—freshly shaved, well-rested and relaxed—looked his age. This despite the premature grayness that had robbed his hair of almost all its original red coloration. He had a lean face with regular features, his coal black eyes and gentle mouthline being the main contributors to his nondescript handsomeness. His frame was small for he stood just a little over five feet six inches and there was no fat to bulk out his compact build.

But all this was merely a first, shallow impression of the man. Ed Craddock had barbered him and inevitably had seen him in close up for a long period. And the desk clerk considered it a part of his job to assess guests in an effort to avoid trouble at the hotel. The clerk had seen Steele ride in off the trail; tired, dirty and hungry. The barber had seen him with a full belly, after a night's solid sleep, cleaned up and dressed up. Steele's attitude had not altered between yesterday and today: but it was, perhaps, from this attitude that both men had reached the same conclusion about the stranger in Friday Wells. Mentally and physically, Adam Steele appeared totally at ease, and yet there was something about him which suggested this was a lie. He smiled a great deal with his mouth, but never with his eyes. They constantly—only apparently without hurry—roved his surroundings. Looking at nothing in particular and seeing everything in detail. And, if they saw a threat, he was instantly prepared to meet it: his loose-limbed, compactly built body poised beneath the phony nonchalance.

Steele was a man familiar with danger and was himself dangerous. As hard as his name and as fast as the action of the rifle which was never out of his reach. The clerk and the barber had seen this and were wary, but Steele had long ago ceased to resent men who showed such a response to him. It was the ones who failed to spot the man under the shell and mistook the shell for the man who were the most likely to rile Steele. And, if they pushed him too far, they got a tough lesson on errors of judgment: often with no life left to learn from their mistakes.

After a short while sitting at the window, Steele began to feel cool and his sweat dried. Outside and below, Friday Wells began to fill with people, the newcomers riding in on horses, buggies and wagons from the four trails that cut across the San Juan Mountains stretch of the Continental Divide to join at the center-town intersection. From his vantage point, the Virginian was able to see across the roofs of the buildings on the other side of the street and watch the steady trickle of traffic heading for town on the north and east trails.

Most of them were farmers and ranchers with their families and hands. Steele had come to Friday Wells on the trail from the north yesterday, riding across rich farm and grazing land spread over the high country of southern Colorado Territory. The encouragement for him to come to the town were the many bills posted to fences and trees over a wide area, proclaiming the Independence Day celebrations in Friday Wells and listing the many events scheduled to take place. One event in particular attracted him—the rifle shooting contest which offered two hundred and fifty dollars to the winner.

This was what he waited for now, able to remain in the room until twelve. Then, because he had no money to pay the rent for another day, he would have to go somewhere else until the contest started at one o'clock.

As the morning progressed, the traffic on the trails lessened to a trickle. The official opening of the celebrations was due at noon and most of those who wanted to join in were already in Friday Wells. The latecomers hurried. A lot of noise was rising from the street—the chatter and laughter of good-humored adults and the squeals and shouts of playful, expectant children.

Steele stood up and leaned forward to look down into the street. Most of the people were moving toward the town square—two blocks down from the hotel—which was formed by the intersection of the trails become streets. On one side of the square, in front of the Crossways Saloon, a wooden platform had been built. It was decked out with flags and colored streamers and a line of chairs had been placed upon it. It was from here that the town's mayor would declare the day's celebration open.

The only people not moving toward the square were the store owners who waited on their premises, anxious for business to resume after the ceremony, and a small group of out-of-towners gathered immediately outside the hotel. Against the background of noise, Steele could hear Billy Cornford delivering a constant stream of boastful talk about his prowess as a fast draw artist. A burst of applause greeted his latest effort and an elderly couple who hurried away from the small group to join the much larger one on the square looked happy with the charcoal sketch the man carried.

But Steele glanced only fleetingly at the people below him. He concentrated his attention on those crowding into the square. But there were too many of them, packed too tightly together as they jostled each other in front of the platform. So he gave up his surveillance, acknowledging to himself that he was unlikely to see the kind of men he was looking for in such a crowd anyway.

There was a knock on the door and the desk

clerk spoke at once. "It's nearly noon, sir! And we have to clean out the room for the next guest."

Steele didn't reply. He put on his jacket, picked up the rifle and took an old, grimy and stained sheepskin coat from the closet. When he pulled open the door, the clerk was about to rap his knuckles on the panel again. The man stepped backward with a startled gasp.

"I hope you've had an enjoyable stay with us, sir," he said quickly. "And that you'll stay with us again when you're next in Friday Wells."

"Grateful for the sentiment," Steele drawled and stepped out on to the balcony. He dropped the key into the clerk's shirt pocket and started down the stairway. The whores were gathered in the lobby doorway, craning their necks outside to look down the street toward the square. The noise had died down as everyone listened to the lone voice of the mayor addressing them. "Pardon me, ladies," the Virginian said as he approached the press of available female bodies blocking the doorway.

"Why, what did you do?" one of the blondes asked with a cruel grin.

Steele halted, wrinkling his nose against the assault of their cheap perfume in the overheated air of the lobby. He had the coat slung over his left shoulder and canted the rifle against the right one.

"Nothin' bad, that's for sure," Clover taunted. "I bet he never even spits and he still says his prayers every night. Spread your wings and fly outta here, angel."

She sidestepped out of the doorway, forcing the other whores to back off. Steele gave a nod and went through the gap, the scent of perfume stronger.

"Make sure you wash behind your ears every day, little angel!" Clover called after him.

Cornford's audience and potential customers had left him to listen to the mayor. The kid, who was about the same height and build as Steele, was smoking a cigarette. His round, freckled face was set in a grin that put a sparkle in his green eyes and parted his lips to show even, very white teeth.

"Here for the shooting match, I guess?" he said easily, nodding toward the sloped Colt Hartford.

"Be the only thing he's shot off since he got to town!" Clover snarled.

"Right, ma'am," Steele agreed, looking toward the square. "I'm aiming for the bull. Never do set my sights on cows."

Clover gasped and made to lunge after Steele. But the other whores held her back.

"Ladies!" the desk clerk shrieked.

All the shade was on the other side of the street and the Virginian crossed to it and sat on an empty beer barrel outside the liquor store. The mayor's voice droned on, seemingly in the same tone as the flies which buzzed in search of scant food. Up on the roof of the brick-built jailhouse across the square from the saloon, two men in the garb of revolutionary soldiers flanked a cannon. When the obese mayor concluded his address, he raised a hand and then dropped it fast. One of the men on the roof touched a taper to the cannon and the charge exploded with a deafening report. A great cheer went up from the crowd packed into the square. Somewhere on the other side of the press of people, a cage was opened and a flock of doves took to the air. The brass and percussion of a band blasted and beat into the opening of a stirring march.

The crowd broke up, men making for the saloon and the women spreading out with their children to give their business to the stores and two restaurants. Steele remained where he was and began to see the kind of men he was looking for. Some of them came out of the Crossways Saloon, having drunk their fill and not liking the abrupt press of new custom. Others rode into Friday Wells, unconcerned with the official trappings surrounding the only event of the celebrations which interested them.

They were the men who would be Steele's prime opponents in the shooting contest—unless one of the local citizens proved to be a talented amateur. From his relaxed position on the barrel, the Virginian counted seven men with the look of the gunslinger about them. Tough, unemotional men with narrowed, unblinking eyes and hands that never strayed far from the butts of revolvers jutting out of tied down holsters. Men who looked at Steele without interest and then did a double-take: recognizing with the second glance one of their own breed.

Like Steele, these men hung around in the shade of sidewalks: aware of what was happening in every direction but with no interest in any of it. And, also like Steele, conscious of the watch being maintained upon them by a man who stood in the doorway of the law office alongside the jailhouse. The Virginian didn't know whether the

11

men were also aware of a more surreptitious surveillance from a less likely quarter—maintained by the green eyes of Billy Cornford.

But the artist's watchfulness was necessarily sporadic, for his abilities were now much in demand: mothers forming a line to have drawings made of their offspring. And these family groups were able to wait in front of the San Juan Hotel without embarrassment, for the whores were no longer in sight. There was nothing overtly shocking about the constant stream of men who moved back and forth between the saloon and the hotel.

Until the bunch of four drunken cowboys dragged a cursing Clover out onto the street. Steele was halfway across the street, intending to get his horse out of the next door livery stable, when the whore's voice screamed an obscenity. She was still in the hotel then and some of the mothers turned and hurried away, attempting to cover the ears of their children. The band, dressed like artillery men in revolutionary soldier's uniform, had marched into the square and were putting their all into martial music. This effectively muffled the scream to all except those immediately in front of the hotel. And, even when the struggling and yelling whore was bundled out into the sunlight, the commotion attracted little attention. For the site of the celebration events was the area fronting the railroad depot at the south end of town and most people were already moving in that direction. Steele had watched the men he considered his competitors head down the street. And he had seen the sheriff amble after them. The first group of women and children went that way, and were hurriedly followed by

12

those who were not driven off until Clover and her tormentors actually showed themselves.

"Let me go, you lousy, stinkin' rotten drunk sons of bitches!" the whore yelled.

She was forced out of the hotel by two laughing men who held each of her arms. Two other men were hard behind the leading trio. One of them had bunched the desk clerk's hair in his hand and was driving the slightly built man into trailing the whore.

"Gentlemen, I implore you!" the desk clerk whined, his lips trembling as he forced out the words.

After a slight pause to see what was happening, Steele continued toward the livery stable entrance. Like his room, the stable had been paid in advance for just the one day. It was now a quarter of one and he was already forty-five minutes in the debt of the liveryman.

"Hold it, mister!" one of the cowboys called. "Stay and watch the show. Best one you'll see in this town today, and completely free!"

Steele halted again and saw the cowboys and their captives clearly now that they were all out of the shade and in the harsh sunlight of early afternoon. He recalled the cowboys from seeing them earlier—a quartet of men in their mid-twenties who he might have considered as possible serious contenders in the shooting match had they not been so drunk. The desk clerk looked more nervous than ever—and with good reason. Clover was angrier than she had ever been toward Steele, this time because of too much attention from men: attention for which they were obviously not paying her.

13

Gone was the paint and powder and the carefully prepared hairstyle. Her face was haggard and deeply lined in the unflattering sunlight, framed by the rat's-tails of her hair. Gone, too, was the red dress she had worn previously. Now she was clothed just in a chemise, patched and dirty, which cupped her bulbous breasts at the top and reached to her knees at the hem.

"I've seen her before," the Virginian answered.

"Stripped naked like she was just born?" the man holding the desk clerk asked.

The band moved off the square, marching down to the events area. Ed Craddock and a few store owners came out on to the sidewalk and were stopped in their tracks by the sight of the near-naked whore and frightened desk clerk struggling for release.

"Let me go, you bastards!" Clover shrieked.

"Please, gentlemen!" the desk clerk begged.

"Gonna get her picture drawn by the one-armed feller here," the man holding the desk clerk went on. "With her little pimp here on top of her. Figure it'll make a fine sign to tack on the hotel door. What d'you think, mister?"

"I don't give a damn what anyone thinks!" Cornford yelled, getting to his feet. "I'm not drawing any dirty picture!"

It was the man unencumbered with a captive who drew his gun. Nobody was looking at him: not even Steele, who had started forward again toward where the liveryman had appeared in the doorway of his stable.

"You'll do it!" he snarled. "And everyone here'll watch it bein' done!" He thrust out his gun hand and pressed the muzzle of the Reming-

14

ton against the sweating temple of the trembling desk clerk. "Anyone tries to stop it and the pimp here gets a hole where his brain oughta be."

None of the cowboys was laughing now. Their spokesman's tone was grimly menacing and the other three took their attitudes from him.

"But why?" the desk clerk managed to rasp out from his fear-constricted throat.

"'Cause this whore tried to lift my billfold while she was puttin' out!"

"That's nothing to do with me!" the desk clerk protested.

"Shuddup!" he was told in a snarl. "You're the pimp for these whores. You get a cut of what they make. Now you're gonna make this one. And you're gonna have your picture done doin' it. And then that picture's gonna get put on the door. And there's gonna be some words underneath. Them words is gonna say—Come to this place to get screwed." His small eyes, besotted with hard liquor, stared out from under the deep ledges of his brows to rake over everyone watching him. He saw shock on the features of the store owners; humor from the whores and their customers looking down from upstairs windows in the hotel façade; defiance from Cornford; and impatience from Steele. He was apparently content with this range of reactions, for a leering smile twisted his mouthline. "Strip 'em down!" he ordered.

The desk clerk, pale and trembling, submitted meekly as the man who had trapped him by the hair started to drag off his jacket. With the Remington pressed against his head, there was little else he could do.

15

Not so Clover. Both her captors released their grip on her arms at the same time, over eager to bare the full-blown body of the whore.

"Blow off his head and hang!" she shrieked, lunging into a run.

Both men grabbed for her, and one managed to hook his curled fingers over the top of the chemise at the back. But it didn't stop her. The old and worn fabric of her underwear parted with a vicious ripping sound. Clover was suddenly naked as she streaked away from the hotel front, her big breasts sagging and swinging and her heavy flanks quivering.

"Don't!" the desk clerk shouted, freezing as motionless as a statue.

To the whore the street abruptly seemed as if it were a mile wide. And, on the other side, she saw the line of store owners drinking in the sight of her abundant nudity. Suddenly she turned and lunged toward the casually standing Steele. He was looking at where one of the cowboys held the desk clerk a prisoner, but he was holding out his coat at arm's length toward her. She skidded to a halt, snatched the coat with a grunt of triumph and draped it around her shoulders, clutching it together at the front to hide her body from throat to midway down her thighs. She had time to snatch a glance at the cowboys then. What she saw in their faces aroused fear from deep inside her and she stepped fast to the side. This put the Virginian between herself and the men.

"Step aside, mister," the leader of the bunch said, his voice soft and evil. "Me and the boys ain't never been known to quit anythin' until we finished it."

His menace was the heaviest. Perhaps because he had his gun drawn against a target he could not possibly miss. But his three partners showed almost the same degree of evil intent. They fastened their steady gazes on Steele's impassive features and their gun hands hovered close to holstered revolvers. They had sobered up but there was no regret about the results of their drinking.

"I want no part of this!" Cornford said into the brittle silence that had followed the cowboy's boast. He stepped forward, between the two easels.

"You'll do as I say," he was told. "Jake, get the woman."

Jake was one of those who had hustled Clover out of the hotel. As he stepped forward, he went for his gun. But the muzzle was not clear of the holster before he was covered. Steele had been holding the rifle ready ever since the whore had run toward him—three fingers curled around the frame, one around the trigger and with his thumb on the hammer. Almost faster than the eye could see, his left hand came up and across his body. At the same time, he flicked the wrist of his right hand and turned his body slightly from the waist. His thumb cocked the hammer and his finger took first pressure against the trigger. The barrel slapped into the cup of his left hand.

"Jesus!" Jake gasped.

He let his gun drop back into the holster. The man at his side and the one behind the desk clerk made to snatch at their guns. But they froze when they saw Jake was covered.

"We're only foolin'," one of them pleaded in a whining tone.

There was an instant of silence. And this time it was not confined to the northern end of the street in front of the hotel. By spontaneous coincidence, the band stopped playing and there was a short lull in the other sounds at the events area. Then:

"She's got to pay!"

The fourth cowboy shrieked these words as he spun, raking his Remington away from the head of the desk clerk toward Steele. There was suddenly a glistening sheen of sweat on his face. The band struck up a new tune. Clover screamed. The desk clerk tried to back away, but tripped on the trailing sleeve of his partially removed jacket. Clover threw herself closer to Steele. The Virginian voiced a low grunt of anger as he was pushed forward by the whore. He was unbalanced and the rifle's aim wavered.

Two revolver shots cracked, the second a split second after the first.

A man was running hard down the street, yelling and brandishing a rifle. He was still on the far side of the square. The sheriff of Friday Wells had not been aware of trouble in front of the San Juan Hotel until he heard the screamed threat end the interval of silence. Nobody in front of the hotel was aware of the lawman's approach.

With one exception, everybody was looking at the revenge-bent cowboy. He was dying, his shot having driven into the ground at his feet, his last wish unfulfilled. Steele only watched him down to his knees, seeing the blood gushing from a wound in his temple to curtain over his cheek. Then the dark eyes of the Virginian, closely followed by

18

the muzzle of the rifle, raked over the survivors. But he had nothing to fear from them. They had snapped their heads around and were staring at their partner as he toppled forward to stretch out at full length in the dust. The dark eyes swiveled further in their sockets. They saw the small black hole in Billy Cornford's advertising sign: then looked at the young artist himself.

Cornford didn't move his feet. Just his one arm—lifting it up to show the Navy Model Colt he was holding. He smiled with grim satisfaction as he rested the still-smoking barrel across the top of the holed sign.

"Just hold every damn thing right there!" This breathless order was barked out by the red-faced sheriff as he lumbered to a panting halt in front of the hotel. His whole body was quivering with anger and exertion and the Spencer rifle he held, inscribed crazy patterns in the air as he waved it from side to side.

But it had the effect of halting the three cowboys as they made to go toward their dead partner.

"He just killed Clifton Reese, sheriff!" Jake announced in an incredulous tone. He pointed a damning finger toward Cornford.

"To keep him from killing the dude," the young artist defended, dropping the smile.

"That's right, Mr. Zuckert!"

"Them four drunks started it!"

"Stripped off Clover!"

"Crazy with the liquor!"

The chorus of support for Cornford came from the whores hanging out of the hotel windows.

"Quiet!" Sheriff Zuckert yelled. "Let's all go

19

into the hotel and get this straightened out."
He glanced over his shoulder toward the distant
celebrations. "No sense in spoilin' other folks'
pleasure."

Steele's expression had not altered from its impassive set from the moment he had been told to
stay and watch the obscene display planned by
Reese. Now, as he returned the rifle hammer to
the rest and sloped the weapon back to his shoulder, he nodded at Cornford and showed a fleeting
puzzled look.

"Grateful to you, mister," he said. "But I could
have handled it myself, I reckon."

"Where the hell do you think you're goin'?" the
sheriff demanded as Steele turned and started on
his way toward the livery.

The Virginian sighed as he halted yet again.
He fixed the lawman with a cold-eyed stare.
"First I'm getting my horse out of the livery," he
replied evenly. "Then I'm going to win some
money in the shooting contest."

The sheriff's fleshy face got redder, the color
shading almost to purple. But he got his shaking
under control and the Spencer was in a rock
steady grip as it was aimed at Steele. "I said everyone in the hotel!" Zuckert barked.

"You got enough people to talk to for a while,
feller," Steele told him. "I'll be back after I've
won the two-fifty I came for."

He continued on across the street and the
liveryman stepped quickly out of the way to allow
him into the stable. He was aware that the
Spencer followed him.

"I'll be back to pay for the extra hour," the
Virginian told the nervous liveryman who

watched him lift down his saddle and gear from the front of a stall.

"How d'you know that, sheriff?" Jake yelled. "He's an accessory to murder."

"I told you, in the hotel!" Zuckert barked, his voice pushed to a high pitch by anger. "All of you!"

The desk clerk was the first to thud his feet on the sidewalk after scrambling up from where he had fallen. Jake and the other two cowboys followed him. Then the storekeepers emerged reluctantly from the shade of their premises and ambled across the street. The liveryman joined them and Steele followed him from the stable, saddle and gear draped over the back of the black gelding. The Colt Hartford was in the saddleboot.

Zuckert's color had almost returned to its natural bronze and his anger was turning from hot to cold as he watched Cornford stand back to usher Clover into the hotel ahead of him.

"I'm allowin' you to go on account you risked a bullet by defyin' me, mister!" the lawman rasped. "Means that two-fifty bucks is mighty important to you."

His bulky form was not primarily fat. He went down onto his haunches, hooked an arm under the limp form of Reese and stood up. He did not even grimace as he lifted the considerable dead weight of the cowboy.

"Grateful to you, feller."

"Just be sure to come back here, that's all!" He spat.

"Got my word," the Virginian promised.

"It's your eyewitness evidence I want, mister."

"And he saw plenty, sheriff," a man called

21

from upstairs in the hotel. He giggled. "That Clover's got plenty to see!"

"Ain't that the naked truth!" another man countered.

From the hotel doorway, the whore looked out at Steele. "Never figured I'd have to say thanks to a guy like you," she said grudgingly. "But thanks."

The Virginian showed a quiet smile. "And I never thought I'd give a whore the coat off my back," he answered.

Chapter Two

They had taken down the corral and pen fencing on the area in front of the railroad depot to provide a broad open space over which to spread the Fourth of July Celebration events. In front of the depot buildings another platform had been raised and the bandsmen were now seated on this, providing a melodious background sound to the din of excitement emanating from elsewhere on the area.

Under flags hanging limply from the tops of high poles, happy people moved this way and that: looking at exhibits which recreated historic incidents, eating and drinking items bought from the refreshment stalls and participating in a wide variety of games of skill and chance.

Steele led the gelding through the press of pleasure-bent people and hitched the reins to a rail at the front of the depot, at the end of the boarding and single line track. Pistol shots began to crack out as he was fastening the cinch but these would be part of the curtain-raising event to the main rifle shooting contest. So he had plenty of time to check the train schedules before drawing the Colt Hartford from the boot and taking two cartons of spare shells from the saddlebag. Then he moved back through the crowds in the area to the east side.

It was here that the major attractions of the afternoon were to be staged. The revolver and rifle shooting contests, the start and finish of the horse race and the rodeo.

Steele got himself a free soda and stood in the shade of the judging tent to watch the hand-gun experts go through their paces. He could handle a revolver, and shoot well with the smaller weapon. But he had not carried one since he was discharged as a cavalry lieutenant from the Confederate army at the end of the War Between the States. He never had claimed to be an expert marksman with anything but a rifle so he was content to be just one of the many spectators at the revolver events.

There were two of them—the straightforward aim and fire at targets spaced out at various distances: and the fast draw and fire. There were twenty entrants for the former and the men who took the first seven places were the only ones who entered the latter. They were the gunslingers Steele had picked out of the crowds earlier. He knew they would not call a halt after the curtain-raiser, for the winner of each event was awarded only twenty-five dollars. And these professional gunmen had not traveled all the way to Friday Wells for that kind of money.

"Guess this is the one you been waitin' for,

24

uh?" the man who had scooped the revolver shooting pool said as he emerged from the judging tent, folding his prize money and tucking it into his shirt pocket.

Like the other six who had trailed him in the scoring, he now carried a rifle. A Winchester that was not very old but the worse for wear.

"I reckon," the Virginian answered, moving forward to join the line of men waiting to register as entrants.

"Sure hope you're a good loser," the tall, thin, black-garbed man called after him. He didn't smile when he said it.

"Even a better winner," Steele said, drawing a pair of black, buckskin gloves from his jacket pocket.

"You'll sure enough win if you can get all that confidence in you down to your trigger finger, Steele."

The Virginian looked over his shoulder at the man who had joined the line behind him. It was Sheriff Zuckert. And he was not the only local man who thought he had a chance with a rifle. The line had grown long with farmers, ranchers, hands and townspeople.

"Told you I'd come by the hotel after this is over, feller," Steele said.

The lawman shook his head. "No need now, mister. Got all the facts I need from the other witnesses. Everyone's in agreement except for Reese's buddies, which is only natural seems to me. Reese was crazy drunk and most likely would have killed you and Miss Clover if'n Billy Cornford hadn't blasted him. And since Reese was in the process of committing the crime of obscenity

25

in the street when he got blasted—well, I don't figure to take the matter no further."

Steele accepted the statement with a nod, but Zuckert laid a restraining hand on his arm as he started to face front again.

"Word of warnin' to you, mister."

"Listening, sheriff."

"Same one I give to Cornford. Jake Whitfield just rode outta Friday Wells. And before he went he said somethin' about Reese, him and their partners being friends of Phil Fish."

Zuckert stared hard into Steele's impassive face, seeking a flicker of recognition for the name. When he saw nothing, the lawman shrugged. "You're a stranger in this part of the territory. Maybe in the whole territory, for I hear tell Phil Fish is known from here to Cheyenne up in Wyoming."

"Not for the good he does, uh?" Steele suggested, leaning to the side to see what was holding things up. The line had not moved since he joined it.

"As the meanest, most cold-blooded killer around. And Jake Whitfield reckons you got as much blame for what happened to Reese as the one-armed kid who killed him."

"Grateful for the warning," Steele said as the mayor, two of the town counselors and the gunslinger dressed in black emerged from the judging tent.

"Stuff about Phil Fish was only half of it," Zuckert said gravely. "Rest of it is to tell you to leave Friday Wells before Fish gets here. Because no matter who blasts who, I'll arrest the one left alive. And he'll stand trial for murder."

"Gentlemen!" the obese mayor yelled, and the gunslinger exploded one of his matched Colts into the air as an added attention-grabber. The mayor gave a nervous nod of thanks for the unsolicited help. "A suggestion has been received to increase the prize money in this event. It has been put to me that the two hundred and fifty dollars donated by the businessmen of Friday Wells be supplemented by a five dollar entrance fee from each contestant. Winner takes all."

The suggestion was greeted with howls of protest and cheers of approval. The swelling crowd of spectators, growing larger as the other events were deserted, added their voices to those in favor. The grinning mayor consulted with the two counselors who were his co-judges and held up his hands for quiet.

"From the volume, it would seem the majority are in favor. Thank you gentlemen."

As he turned, amid a further burst of cheers and howls, the gunslinger in black extended a five-spot bill. The mayor accepted this first contribution to the increased pot and he and the town councilors went into the tent.

"Kinda leaves you feelin' like I was this mornin', don't it dude?"

Joe, the drunk who had tried to beg a handout from Steele earlier, grinned at the Virginian from out of the crowd. He had been a lot luckier in touching others for money. For his filthy face was highly colored from liquor and he was clutching an almost full bottle to his chest.

Steele ignored Joe as one of the men in front of him dropped out. He glanced back along the line and saw two others retire. A number of other contestants scowled their displeasure, but stayed in line. Steel had not seen the gunslinger re-enter the tent, but he saw him emerge. He was carrying a square of white cardboard, which he pinned at the side of the tent entrance. The lettering was scrawled but big and plain to read: CASH ON THE LINE ONLY. NO MARKERS ACCEPTED. YOU GOT TO PAY TO PLAY.

"You as broke as you don't look?" the sheriff asked as the line started forward, the men who had registered emerging from the rear of the tent.

"You wouldn't be reckoning to stake me, sheriff?" Steele asked softly.

Zuckert made a sound of disgust. "I sure wouldn't mister. You drop out, that's one guy less I got to beat. And a guy who don't carry no handgun—just a rifle—well, seems to me that guy's just gotta be pretty good with a rifle."

Steele remained in the line as it shuffled forward, his gloved hands wrapped tightly around the rifle. Apart from memories and the hard-learned lessons in survival, the buckskin gloves were all he had brought out of the war. He could not recall at what precise point he had come to regard them as lucky omens. He knew only that they were prized possessions, second only in importance to the engraved Colt Hartford: which was the sole material asset he had inherited from his brutally murdered father.

He was inside the judging tent now, standing before a trestle table behind which sat the grossly overweight mayor flanked by the two town counselors. One of the counselors was taking the entrance money while the other registered the name of each contestant. The mayor simply sat and beamed, obviously highly satisfied with the way the celebrations in Friday Wells were progressing.

"Name?"

"Adam Steele."

The town councilor entered it at the foot of a list on one sheet of paper and then scribbled a receipt on a small piece.

"Hand Mr. Post your five dollars, sir."

"Reckon to put up my rifle instead of money," Steele drawled.

The mayor stopped beaming. All three civic dignitaries glared at Steele.

"You saw the sign outside," Post snapped. "No credit against markers. That includes material collateral." He grinned around Steele. "Afternoon, sheriff. You'll show a few of these youngsters how to shoot, uh?" Post got the scowl back on his face as he glanced at Steele again. "Pay up or move on, will you. We're already running behind schedule."

The Virginian knew he would have to accept the ruling. He had tried to get around it and failed.

"Move on, dude."

"Get outta here."

"Let's get the damn show started."

As the men behind Zuckert growled their impatience, Steele turned away from the table. His regular features betrayed no sign of disappointment. Anger would have been futile and trouble pointless. Then something small and dark arced through the air from the tent's rear exit and thudded on the table. It didn't bounce. It simply jingled as it settled where it fell. A spotted neckerchief tied with a leather thong.

"Nothin' in the rules about one guy stakin' another," Billy Cornford said as he stepped into view. "Take five bucks out of there and let me have what's over."

"Guess that'll be all right," the mayor said quickly, grabbing the makeshift money bag and unfastening the thong.

The town counselor finished writing out the receipt and handed it to Steele. Steele waited until the five dollars in loose coins had been counted out, then picked up the much lighter neckerchief and handed it back to the youngster as he went outside.

"All you get is the five bucks back out of my winnings," he said coldly.

"Did I ask for anythin' else?" Cornford responded evenly.

"I didn't ask for anything."

Cornford shrugged as he pushed the neckerchief and its contents into his pants pocket. "You're the kind of guy who never asks for a thing, Steele. And you ain't a taker, either." Another shrug, but with a bright grin to accompany it this time. "I figure you for a winner, though. When you get a fair shake."

He started to return to where his two easels were set up with the folding chair behind one of them. A large group of people were waiting to have their portraits sketched.

"Oh, Steele!" the artist called as the Virginian turned to move away from the tent. "My horse is hitched next to yours over at the depot. Your coat's strapped to him. Clover said to tell you thanks again." His grin broadened. "Said you really are a regular angel, even if she never saw you spread your wings."

"How about that, Steele," the sheriff said with a leer as he emerged from the judging tent. "Made yourself right popular with one of our local ladies of ill repute."

"She's confusing wings and flies, feller," Steele muttered. "When she sees a man she just can't get her thoughts on to higher things."

The soda stall was still dispensing free drinks and Steele helped himself to another while he waited for the rifle shooting match to start. Then the registration process was finished and the mayor and town counselors called all the entrants to the edge of the area. Fifty-eight riflemen had paid their five dollars to raise the prize money to five hundred and forty. Not a fortune, but enough to create a great deal of excitement among the spectators and a number of the contestants.

The fat mayor called a halt to the music and started in on what could have been another long speech.

"Cut the spiel, fatso!" the gunslinger in black interrupted when the mayor paused for breath after enthusing about the kind of crack shot a man would have to be to win. "Let's get on with the action."

The mayor scowled, but his expression quickly changed to a placating beam as shouts were raised in agreement with the gunslinger.

"All right, all right, ladies and gentlemen!" the mayor yelled, waving his arms about to bring silence. "Men'll be called to the line six at a time in the order they registered. One shot apiece at the targets out there. Bulls will go forward into a next shoot out. Keep on like that until we whittle down to a winner."

The targets he spoke of were placed a hundred yards out in a field to the north of the depot stockyard area. There were six of them comprised of circles within circles printed on three-by-three pieces of white board propped against wooden supports. Parked to one side was a buckboard loaded with fresh target boards and manned by two more town counselors. Two young boys in their early teens stood beside the buckboard, ready to bring back the used targets after each volley of shots had been fired.

As shooting matches went, Steele considered this one was quite well organized. And he had entered many during his formative years in prewar Virginia, winning more than he lost. But, in those days, the competition had not been so tough. Mostly rich plantation owners or the sons of rich plantation owners like himself. Men who knew guns and the effects which wind and weather could have on particular shots and various kinds of bullets. But men who had only ever fired their guns when hunting or in such competitions. Skilled in the art of shooting, but not of killing.

The first six names were called and the men moved up to their marks opposite the targets. Four local people and two of the professional gunmen. They fired from whichever position they chose and three of them scored bulls.

Shooting and killing were two entirely different things. In simple shooting, a man could miss and be sure to go on living. When he was killing, it was invariably in order to survive. The war had changed Steele from a crack shot into a survivor with a gun. And, in the violent peace which events had forced upon him in the wake of the war, he had developed his ability to survive against those who attempted to kill him. To the extent that now he shot with instinct and reflex, without needing to think about what he did. From this came his confidence. It was his habit not to miss: and habits died hard. This one kept him living.

In the next group of six, two placed their shots in the center of the targets. Both were professionals.

Steele was called as one of the next group, and the shouting of his name rose a stir of excitement from the eager audience. He could guess why. In a small town like Friday Wells, news traveled fast: and the fact that it was July Fourth would not alter this. People would know about his involvement in the shooting outside the San Juan Hotel. They would know that his dudish appearance was a façade for being flat broke. They would have heard about his confident determination to win.

He took up his position and Sheriff Zuckert moved into line beside him. When the name Bob Porter was yelled, the gunslinger in black joined the group.

"Fire at will, gentlemen!" the mayor yelled after he had checked that the men and boys out in the field had moved to the wagon.

Steele and Porter responded at once. Porter was sightly ahead, for his Winchester was already aimed from the hip. Steele had to flip his forward from the shoulder. He squeezed the trigger as the barrel was grasped by his gloved hand. The sheriff dropped on to one knee and sighted from the shoulder. The three farmhands who completed the group went out prone.

The targets were collected by the boys, who ran back with them to the mayor. The fat man disqualified two of the farmhands from continuing.

"Good mister," Porter growled as they made way for the next men to fire. He hardly parted his lips to display a hard, tight smile. His glittering blue eyes were faintly taunting. "And we're goin' to find out just how good after the chaff gets shot outta the wheat, right?"

As the remainder of the contestants were called forward and blasted at the targets, the crowd of spectators began to drift away. The initial stages of the shooting match were too easy and lacked excitement. The band struck up again and the other attractions in front of the depot began to recapture attention.

Billy Cornford did as well as any other showman on the events area, quickly recouping the five dollars he had staked to Steele. And he remained busy even between his paying customers—his single, talented hand sketching lightning pictures of his surroundings.

Steele stood in the shade of the judging tent, inviting no conversation from those around him. And he showed no interest in anything except the contest, watching each entrant as he took his position on the line and then shifting his gaze to the targets. By the time that the first round was over, he had added three more men to the seven who would give him strong competition. Two of them looked like farmhands and the other was a smartly dressed rancher. Although they lacked the easy relaxation of the gunslingers, they had the same dedication to what they were doing. They wanted to win and enjoying themselves had nothing to do with it.

For the second round, the targets were moved back fifty yards and there were thirty men left to shoot. Sheriff Zuckert was one of the sixteen who didn't make it through to the third round.

The afternoon was more than an hour older from when the contest had started and the sun was as hot as it ever had been since midmorning. Children had become fretful with the heat and the waning of their interest in the celebrations. Parents lost their tempers with their whining young. Men with no family commitments moved back along the street to drink in the coolness of the Crossways Saloon, or to work up a different kind of sweat with the whores in the San Juan Hotel.

But the reduced field in the shooting match began to spark new interest and Ed Craddock, the town barber, added to this. He had been watching the first two rounds with as much interest as Steele and, as the names of those through to the third round were called, he started to offer betting odds on the successful fourteen. Word of this spread fast across the depot area and then into town. People flocked into a crowd that swelled. The band stopped playing again and became spectators.

The targets were shifted back yet another fifty yards, which placed them on higher ground for the field sloped up on the east side of the valley in which Friday.Wells was set.

"You look like a guy that don't worry much about anythin'," Billy Cornford said as he moved into the shade of the tent, carrying the tools of his trade under his good arm.

"So tell me about it," the Virginian offered.

Cornford grinned, the expression crinkling the freckled flesh around his blue eyes. "I made twenty bucks today. Not counting the five I staked you. Just put the whole bundle on you to win."

Steele nodded. "What odds did you get, feller?"

"Three-to-one."

"Law officer has to be a careful man," Zuckert put in as he joined them in the shade. "I've got five on Porter. Even money." He mopped at his sweating face with a damp neckerchief. "Two other shooters are at evens."

"Been a long time since I was anybody's favorite," Steele said as he moved out into the direct sunlight as his name was called by the mayor.

"We're both of us outsiders, Steele!" Cornford shouted after him.

At the line, the Virginian was flanked by Porter and the rancher.

"I been wondering about that name of yours," the gunslinger said softly, moistening his thumb and forefinger and touching the dampness to the foresight of his Winchester.

"It bother you, feller?"

Porter clicked his tongue against the roof of his mouth. He shook his head. "Just find it strange I ain't heard of you. Feller that can shoot good as you, word usually gets around."

"Fire at will, gentlemen!" the mayor announced.

This invitation caused a silence to descend upon the tight press of spectators. Two of the gunslingers squeezed off shots immediately, standing erect but with their rifle stocks against their shoulders. The rancher went down on one knee and fired. A farmhand stretched out on his belly and his rifle exploded a second later. Groans from the shooters and a portion of the crowd greeted four misses.

"You'll be able to start the word on its way," the Virginian invited as he raised the Colt Hartford.

"If you do anythin' worth talkin' about," Porter said, staring hard at Steele.

He saw the buckskin stretch tight over the knuckle of the trigger finger. Then he coughed. Distance didn't make it a difficult shot, so much as that the targets were on higher ground. The sound of Porter's cough was covered by the report of the rifle.

A burst of applause signified a good hit but there was no satisfaction on the Virginian's face as he lowered the rifle and turned.

"You want to take care of that bad throat, feller," he said. "It could develop into something fatal."

Porter was as fast as he was accurate. He slammed the stock of the Winchester into his shoulder, slapped his cheek against the side and squeezed the trigger. Smooth and easy. He pumped the action as he jerked the rifle down, against a background of even wilder applause.

"I take good care of every part of me," he replied with a twisted grin.

They split, Steele to return to where Cornford and Zuckert stood by the tent and Porter going over to Craddock. Some of the money he had won with his revolver was given to the barber. Craddock got even more business as those who had bet on the losers put out more money.

"That guy tried to put you off, didn't he, Steele?" Cornford asked, a little anxiously.

The Virginian showed a tight smile as he ejected the three spent shell cases from the rifle chambers and reloaded. "Obviously doesn't know what you know about me and worry, feller."

"You want to lodge a complaint with the judges?" Zuckert asked grimly. "Mayor Hammond may be an old windbag, but he's a fair man."

Steele eyed Zuckert levelly. "Grateful, sheriff, but I make it a general rule to handle my own trouble."

The next six men fired and two gunslingers hit the bull. The final two men failed. Anxious to keep excitement high, Mayor Hammond called the final four shooters to the line immediately. But there was a necessary delay while the targets were pushed a further fifty yards up the hill. Gambling men jostled around the town barber, thrusting bills at him and shouting the names of the shooters they favored.

The town streets were deserted now and every building was empty. Somebody—perhaps Zuckert —had started the story that Porter was worried by Steele and was trying to cheat. But the tension between them did not show through the calm façades of the men themselves. It was all generated from within the crowd.

"Quiet down there!" the mayor yelled. "Men like these don't like no distractions when they're shootin'."

It took several seconds for a new silence to clamp down over the crowded side of the events area.

"You know what to do, gents," the mayor invited. "Any time you like."

"Jake oughta be back pretty soon with Phil Fish," a familiar voice muttered from the crowd.

"Then there'll be some real shooting," came the reply.

Steele didn't have to turn around. He knew the comments had been made by the two cowboys who had stayed in Friday Wells after Whitfield rode out.

"Quiet, I said!" Mayor Hammond snarled.

None of the men at the line had raised their rifles.

"Phil Fish is a name I know real well," Porter said softly. "Well as I know my own and them of Gus Young and Chuck Burton here. Guys with reps get known."

Steele's shot punctuated Porter's final comment. The Virginian's style was the same as always—flicking his wrist to take the Colt Hartford away from his shoulder, cocking it in the same

39

action. Then, with no pause, raising the stock into his shoulder, sighting, and squeezing the trigger. But the speed of the move was faster than anything he had shown in the contest so far. It took everybody by surprise, including the three gunslingers. As the crowd seemed to gasp with one voice, Steele withdrew from the line without a second glance at the distant target.

"Steele with an "e" at the end," the Virginian told his startled competitors.

Porter was suddenly angry, but he got control of himself. He was as fast as Steele, and as cool.

"Another winner!" a man yelled from the crowd. "Right in the damn center, by God!"

Sunlight glinted on the lenses of the binoculars as he pulled them from his eyes. Young and Burton waited for the noise of excitement to die, then took their time with the shots. With the exception of Steele and Porter, everyone looked hard at the man with the binoculars. He shook his head as he lowered the glasses.

"Misses, I'd say."

"We'll wait for official confirmation," Mayor Hammond tried to announce, but his pompous tones were lost amid the noise of the crowd as Ed Craddock offered even money on both finalists.

"What now?" Porter asked the mayor as the two boys came racing back with the used targets.

The fat man blinked. "Another fifty yards back, I guess."

Porter shook his head and jerked a thumb at Steele. "Don't waste our time, mister. Him and me can hit anythin' over any distance long as we can see it and it's standin' still. Tie a couple of targets to the back of that buckboard and have someone whip the horses into a gallop."

The mayor shook his head vigorously. "Far too dangerous. I cannot allow—"

"Mr. Hammond! Sheriff!" The shout came from inside the judging tent. A man's voice which was loud and strident with anxiety. The still-noisy crowd caught the timbre of the voice and all sound was abruptly curtailed. Every pair of eyes swung toward the tent. There was just a single scream from a woman as Post, one of the organizing town counselors, staggered out through the entrance flaps. He was hatless and a zigzagged pattern of dried blood decorated one side of his face from a discolored area on his temple. He made five yards down the human corridor formed by the dividing crowd, then his legs collapsed from under him and he pitched to the ground.

But he stayed conscious behind his pain-glazed eyes. "The money!" he croaked. "Two men! They took it! Kerchiefs over their faces! Hit me!"

A babble of talk erupted from the crowd. A shot ended it and all eyes swung toward Steele. The Virginian held his rifle high in the air, one-handed. Smoke curled from its muzzle.

"Be grateful if you folks would stay quiet," he said, an expression of tense concentration on his face.

All of those whose ears were not effected by age, heard the sound which had captured Steele's attention. Hoofbeats at the gallop. Already diminished by great distance and becoming less audible by the moment.

"I don't hear nothin'!" somebody growled.

"Over to the south!" Porter snapped. "Out along the railroad!"

It was he who took the lead, with Steele hard behind him. Post was in danger of being trampled underfoot as the crowd parted to open up another corridor. Then closed it again and chased after the two men with rifles. Porter and Steele broke into the open and sprinted across to the depot building and around the side to halt on the track. The sun-glinting rails ran in a perfectly straight line down the center of the long valley. Featureless slopes of grassland swept up on either side of the strip of cinders supporting the track. Two horsemen were heeling their mounts into a flat out gallop alongside the track on the west side. They were a half mile out from the depot.

"I'm takin' one of these horses!" Zuckert gasped breathlessly as he forced a way through the crowd, saw the galloping men and swung to where the geldings of Steele and Cornford were hitched.

"No need for that, sheriff," Porter said. "Me and Steele can take care of them guys. Maybe figure out which of us is the best shot at the same time."

"No you damn well won't!" Zuckert snarled, turning from the horses and draping a hand over his holstered sixgun. "This is law business. And ain't no proof them two guys stole the money."

Neither the Virginian nor the gunslinger looked at the lawman. Both stared out along the railroad track as the runaways diminished in size by perspective.

"Okay, Steele?" Porter asked.

"I said no!" Zuckert yelled.

Steele cocked the hammer of the Colt Hartford. "Call it, feller," he invited.

There was utter silence again. Not even hoof-beats now, for the men were too far off.

"You take the one on the left. One on the right's mine. First to fire is the loser if we both make hits."

"Killing shots?"

Porter spat and grinned as he raised the Winchester to his shoulder. "I figure that's my money, mister. And I don't take kindly to gettin' robbed."

Steele responded by easing the stock of the Colt Hartford against his shoulder and lining up the two sights. The surrounding silence seemed to have a physical presence that pressed down through the air, making it hotter and heavier. The smell of sweating bodies was strong in everyone's nostrils.

"Take it easy, sheriff," Mayor Hammond counseled with unusual authority. "No reason for those men to take off the way they did unless they got more than a fast ride on their minds."

"One of you shoot, for Christ sake!" Ed Craddock yelled.

Steele was like a statue, not a muscle moving. His eye did not wander from the aligned sights of the rifle. But he could sense the cracking nerve of Porter. Felt the gunslinger's eyes as they constantly flicked from the target to his opponent. He heard a small bone in the man's leg crack.

Then the Winchester exploded, a much louder sound. The distance was more than three-quarters of a mile but the light was good and there was no wind or dust. Everyone watching saw the horseman on the right sway in his saddle as the other man glanced over his shoulder. The cheer which had started was cut short as the wounded horseman stayed in the saddle.

"Bastard!" Porter snarled, and made the mistake of getting angry at himself. He pumped the action of the Winchester and squeezed off another shot. Then again, and again and a third time. And still he did not stop. The rifle stayed up and aimed until the firing pin clicked into an empty breech.

"Fat chance I got of catchin' them now!" Zuckert snarled as he swung his bulky frame up into the saddle of Cornford's gelding.

"Sonofabitch!" Porter growled, hurling his Winchester into the dust.

Steele blew on a fly that had settled on the tip of his trigger finger. The fly took wing with an angry buzz. The finger squeezed the trigger. The uninjured horseman tipped forward against the neck of his mount and then rolled off the galloping animal. Before he hit the ground Steele had raked the rifle barrel an inch to the right and fired another shot. This man was already leaning to the side as he was hit. He threw his arms high into the air and fell cleanly from his saddle.

"Man, he don't just shoot off his mouth, does he?" somebody asked rhetorically.

"You guys better hope I find five forty bucks out there!" Zuckert growled as he wheeled the gelding and heeled him into a gallop out along the railroad track.

"We got us a winner, folks!" Mayor Hammond yelled, the familiar bouncy tone in his voice.

But nobody paid any attention to him. The

44

crowd was split, half the people peering out along the valley after Zuckert and the rest milling around the harassed Ed Craddock.

"You done it fair and square, Steele," Porter said grudgingly, with no friendliness on his long, thin face as he extended a hand toward the Virginian. "I'll remember you."

He towered head and shoulders over Steele. The Virginian had the Colt Hartford held low across the front of his body. As he went forward, apparently to accept the proferred handshake, he moved into a sudden pivot. The rifle stock arced in under Porter's outstretched arm and smacked into the gunslinger's belly. Porter's breath was expelled with a *whooooosh* and he started to bend forward. Steele jerked up the rifle barrel. The muzzle connected with the point of Porter's jaw. The gunslinger was forced erect again, a snarl of rage following the rasp of escaped air. By the time his hands touched the butts of his sixguns, the Colt Hartford was cocked and aimed at him.

The crowd had fallen back at the first sign of trouble. Now they formed a tight-packed arc around Porter and Steele. Silence had succeeded noise again. Except for the beat of hooves as Zuckert rode out into the valley: and the scratching of charcoal against paper.

"What the—?" Porter started.

Steele forced a cough. "I did it, is all, feller," he said.

"Now then, now then!" the fat mayor said placatingly. "No more trouble, please. This is a happy day." He climbed up on to a stack of crates in front of the depot building. "All entrants in the horse race to assemble at the start, ladies and

45

gentlemen. Lots of fun to be had and money to be won."

But nobody was ready for anything else until Porter had dropped his hands from his sixguns, turned and scooped up the empty Winchester.

"It didn't bother you, none, Steele," the gunslinger muttered.

Steele shouldered the rifle and showed a quiet grin as he massaged his own jaw. "Bothered you more, I guess."

Even with the tension of the standoff past, the crowd still did not disperse. Everybody waited at the end of the railroad track until Zuckert rode back, leading two horses with the dead riders slumped across their backs. Both had taken bullets just below their left shoulder blades. One of them had a wound lower down. The spilled blood was already dry as swarms of flies raked at it.

One of the saddle bags on Cornford's gelding was open. The sheriff dug into it and produced a stack of bills held together by a rubber band. He tossed the bundle of money at Steele, who caught it and pushed it into a jacket pocket.

"Stay a winner, Steele," he advised. "Get out of Friday Wells before Phil Fish gets here."

The Virginian had tilted his head to one side in order to look at the upside-down faces of the dead men. They were the first pair of professional gunmen to get disqualified from the shooting match.

"You already told me, sheriff," he said as he straightened and turned away from the bodies. "I'll be leaving on the six o'clock train."

"Phil oughta be here before then," one of the cowboys said from the crowd, which parted to allow Steele a passage.

Billy Cornford interrupted his sketching of the dead men on the horses to grin brightly at Steele.

"Grateful to you, feller," the Virginian told him, peeling off five one dollar bills and pressing them into the youngster's shirt pocket.

"Likewise," Cornford countered. "My twenty won me sixty and I got you to thank, Steele."

"Then you'll both be able to afford high-class funerals for yourselves when Phil Fish gets here!" one of the cowboys yelled.

"This guy Fish must really be somethin' special," Cornford said, still grinning.

"You just wait and see!" the cowboy taunted.

"I'll do that, feller," the Virginian replied quietly. "With bated breath."

Chapter Three

Sheriff Zuckert returned Cornford's horse to the hitching rail, then yelled for the town's mortician and the both of them led the two corpse-burdened horses along the main street to the Friday Wells Funeral Parlor. Steele was not long in following them, after first finding the liveryman. He paid for the extra hour of stabling and added some money to take care of feed and water until the evening train arrived.

Behind him as he strolled down to the square of the cross streets, the area in front of the railroad depot became noisy and full of movement again. The remaining events of the celebrations got under way and the static attractions began to engender interest again. But there was less excitement quivering in the hot afternoon air.

Steele was unaware of just how hot it was until he entered the batwings doors of the Crossways Saloon. He had tried both restaurants first, but they were closed up while the people who ran

48

them joined in the celebrations. There were two bartenders behind the long bar that ran along one wall of the murky, cool saloon. Steele was the only customer.

"Can you fix coffee and something to eat?" he asked as he bellied up to the bar, resting the rifle along the polished top.

"It ain't usual," the elder and fatter of the two said flatly.

"It's an unusual day," the Virginian replied.

"Sure is," the younger and thinner one agreed. Despite their differences, there was a certain family resemblance about them. Probably brothers. "Ain't three people ever died in one day in Friday Wells since the fever epidemic. When was that, Irwin?"

"First year of the war, Drew."

"Anyone ever die here from hunger?" Steele asked, taking off his gloves and flexing his sweat-tacky fingers.

"Oughta be some coffee in the pot on the stove, Drew. And fix the man a meat loaf sandwich."

"Grateful to you," Steele said, and laid a dollar bill on the bar top.

"Poor fare for what could be a man's final meal," Sheriff Zuckert growled as he pushed through the batwings.

"Thought you were going to stop it, feller," the Virginian said without turning around, as Irwin pulled a foaming glass of beer without being asked.

"Gonna try," the lawman allowed, reaching the bar ten feet from where Steele stood.

The beer was sent spinning along the bar top

toward him with only a little froth being spilled. He sucked up half of it with noisy relish.

"But I certainly ain't no match for you, mister. And from what I've heard about Phil Fish, he shoots his pearl-handled Tranter even better than you handle that there rifle."

Drew emerged from a bead-hung archway behind the bar and placed the coffee and sandwich in front of Steele. The dollar was clawed away and no change was given. Steele started in on the sandwich.

"If Fish is so good, why wasn't he here for the shooting, sheriff?"

"Handgun man. And what was up for prize money in that match is chicken feed to Fish. Hear tell he never draws his gun unless there's a grand on the line."

"Whitfield and his buddies rich cowpunchers?"

Zuckert grimaced as he finished his beer and spun back the empty glass for a refill. "Whitfield, Hart and Burke probably couldn't raise the price of a beer anytime except pay day. Reese was a tightwad, which was why he took being rolled by the whore so hard, I guess."

"Thousand dollar mean?"

Another grimace greeted the fresh beer. "Just a cowboy like the others. But it seems Phil Fish used to run with 'em before he got to be a gun for hire. Real good friends."

The sheriff took his second beer in one swallow and slapped some coins on the bar top. He glanced at Steele as the Virginian munched on the sandwich, seemed about to say something else but decided against it. He swung around and made for the batwings.

"Appreciate somethin', Mr. Zuckert!" Irwin called.

"What's that?"

"If you'd remind some of them folks down at the depot about how good our beer tastes. Especially on a hot day like this."

"They'll be comin' down the street soon," the lawman said sourly. "Things are seemin' kinda dull over there now the main event's done."

He went out and, after the doors had ceased creaking behind him, a pleasant silence filled the cool and murky saloon. Irwin and Drew had nothing to say to each other and Steele was content with his own thoughts as he finished the meager meal. Then, when he had eaten, he nodded to the two bartenders and left the saloon.

Across the square, the door of the law office was open wide and the bulky form of the sheriff could just be discerned, hunched in a chair behind the desk. Steele turned toward the quiet end of the street and his footfalls echoed hollowly on the sidewalk boarding. For a while, he sat on the barrel outside the liquor store, but the sun was well on its way down the western dome of the sky now and there was no shade on this side of the street.

As he rose and crossed to the San Juan Hotel, Zuckert's prediction began to be proved correct. People were leaving the events area and heading along the street. The sounds of enjoyment were more subdued as the celebration attractions lost their novelty. Steele stepped over the dull bloodstain in the dust left by Clifton Reese and went up onto the sidewalk and into the hotel lobby.

"They're all in their rooms, Mr. Steele," the slightly built clerk announced as the Virginian

51

glanced around. "You're welcome to wait here in the lobby until train time." He showed a nervous smile. "They'll sleep until some new customers show up. You'll be left alone."

Steele had considered renting a room for what was left of the afternoon, but one of the bulging chesterfields in the lobby seemed like a good, free resting place.

"Grateful to you," he said as he sat down. As the upholstery was compacted beneath him, it gave off a brief whiff of cheap perfume.

"Least I can do after what you and the one-armed kid did for me this noon time. It could have been most embarrassing."

"You know anything about Cornford?" Steele asked, glancing at the clock hung on the wall above the desk. It showed the time at four o'clock.

The clerk blinked. "Nothing, Mr. Steele. He rode into Friday Wells early and asked permission to set up outside the hotel. He was most polite. Drew my picture for nothing."

Steele brought an end to the conversation by leaning his head back and tipping his hat forward over his eyes. The one-armed artist intrigued him. He was always around when trouble hit. He had taken a liking to Steele. He had made the comment about them being similar—both "outsiders." He could handle the Navy Colt as good as—maybe better—than the gunslingers. Steele had seen him draw it in an instant and make a killing head shot from the hip and when firing through the obstruction of his advertising sign. Luck had played no part in it.

"What's that?" Steele asked suddenly from under his hat.

The clerk was jerked out of a mental reverie and looked at the Virginian with surprise. Then he heard it. A regular hammering sound from out back of the hotel.

"The mortician," he supplied. "His workshop is behind the San Juan. Busy day for him today. Fixing the boxes for the dead men."

"This is what he looks like."

Cornford's voice was the first announcement that he had entered the hotel. As Steele pushed his hat squarely atop his head he realized this was an aspect of the artist he had overlooked in his tally of the youngster. He was a silent mover.

The kid was standing on the lobby threshold, holding up one of his sketches, the black charcoal lines on white card depicted a gaunt-looking man hammering nails into an elongated box. Three similar boxes were stacked to one side. On the other side of the mortician, three shrouded bodies were stretched out.

"Seems Reese's buddies Hart and Burke ordered the fourth one made," Cornford said with his easy grin. "Mortician has another one to do for them." The grin broadened. "Or should I say for us?"

"How about Clover?" Steele asked.

Cornford gave his lopsided shrug. "Maybe Fish is the kind that won't go up against a woman."

Footfalls thudded on the sidewalk outside. "I'm sure ready to go up against one," a man slurred; and laughed as he reeled in around Cornford. "If you know what I mean?"

It was the sharpshooting rancher, who had drowned his sorrows in the saloon and was now happy at the prospect of buying himself one of the San Juan girls. But his expression soured as his glazed eyes swept the lobby and failed to see what he wanted.

"Hot damn!" he growled. "A cat house with no pussy!"

"Upstairs, sir," the desk clerk directed. "Any door with the number in red."

"Woweee!" the rancher yelled as he started across the lobby. "Let me at 'em!"

He took the stairs two at a time. Cornford went out of the hotel, but only to get his two easels, folding chair and supply of paper board and finished drawings. "Take care of these will you?" he asked the clerk, leaning his stuff against the front of the desk. "That guy has given me an idea how to kill the time before the train leaves. A big idea."

He laughed as he followed the rancher up the stairs. At the top he stopped and looked down into the lobby. "How about it, Steele?" he called happily.

The Virginian's face was back under the tilted hat. "Only ride I plan today is aboard the train," he drawled in reply.

"All work and no play, Steele."

"Poker's my game."

Cornford laughed. "Pardon me while I indulge in a little stud of my own," he called as he crossed the balcony. "With an ace in the hole!"

The desk clerk made tutting sounds with his tongue. "The class of people at the San Juan has certainly gone down since the management introduced the ladies," he commented bitterly.

"How about the take?" Steele asked sleepily.

"No complaints," the clerk admitted.

"Except the kind your customers take across to the town doc, I guess," the Virginian muttered.

He didn't go to sleep. Rather, he dozed fitfully, kept close to alertness by the steady flow of men who entered the lobby and were directed upstairs by the reluctantly eager clerk. And he was able to make an accurate assessment of the passage of time: to the extent that when he stood up, stretched and looked at the clock he found he was only five minutes fast in his guess at a quarter of six.

The air was noticeably cooler and the sunlight out on the street had a red tinge to it. The clerk directed a nervous-looking, business-suited, middle-aged man up the stairway, then smiled at Steele.

"My thanks again, sir," he said. "And I trust you will be able to leave Friday Wells without further unpleasantness. Should I call down Mr. Cornford?"

Steele was pulling on the black gloves. Then he picked up the Colt Hartford and canted it to his shoulder. "If his mind's set on catching the train, he'll catch it," he said as he started for the door.

He stepped out on to the sidewalk and breathed in deeply of the evening air. A slight breeze was curling in over the eastern rim of the valley and making slow time down the slope to brush through the town. Not strong enough to lift any dust: but it stirred the smoke from chimneys and swayed the flags on the high poles in front of the railroad depot. The area the flag poles surrounded was now deserted. The main street and those which went off from the square to the east and west were uncrowded. Most of the family people who had come into Friday Wells for the Independence Day celebrations had left. Many of the stores were closed.

As Steele turned to stroll along the sidewalk, he could hear a buzz of talk against a background of piano music coming from the Crossways Saloon. The two restaurants were both about half-full. The smell from them was good. From far off, beyond the south end of the valley, came the plaintive wail of a locomotive whistle.

Sheriff Zuckert stepped out of the law office doorway as Steele started across the intersection forming the square. He held his rifle in a two-handed grip across his bulging belly.

"Been a long afternoon," the sheriff said, falling in beside Steele. "Mind if I walk down to the depot with you?"

"Your town, feller."

Zuckert spat into the dust ahead of him and glanced sourly to either side of him. "Look at 'em! Just itchin' for Phil Fish to get here before the train pulls out."

The Virginian was already aware that he was a center of attention again. He and the lawman had moved out into the center of the south stretch of the main street. A lot of men and some women were on the flanking sidewalks, watching in silence: a silence that extended to the saloon. For the moan of the train whistle had brought the piano music to an end. The sound of voices had continued until the former patrons of the saloon had jostled out into the square. They now formed a moving crowd of more than a score of men trailing Steele and Zuckert.

56

"Look at you yellow-bellies!" Hart taunted from one side of the street.

"Yeah!" Burke countered from the opposite side "Takin' it on the lam before Fish can get here."

Steele took note of the plural pronoun and he shot a fast glance over his shoulder. Just ahead of the crowd from the saloon was the grinning Billy Cornford, his slight form canted to the side by the burden of his equipment.

The train whistle blew again. High in the darkening sky, above and far beyond the depot building, a cloud of black wood smoke billowed and swirled.

"You're a man of extreme patience, Steele," Zuckert said with a note of admiration.

The Virginian curled back his lips in a quiet smile. "It may be my only virtue," he replied.

"I doubt that, son," the lawman said.

Steele glanced to left and right and behind him again. But his casual attitude was false for his dark, narrowed eyes noted every face they swept over. "You see Porter and the other guns ride out, sheriff?" he asked.

Zuckert was overtly concerned as he made a survey of his own. "Sure didn't. Saw the whole bunch of 'em go into the saloon a while back. Ain't seen 'em since."

Cornford caught up with Steele on the other side of him from Zuckert. There was no sound of his proximity until he spoke. "You ain't startin' to worry, are you, Steele?" he asked lightly.

"Hate for you to lose your faith in me," the Virginian told him, resting his thumb on the hammer of the Colt Hartford.

"No chance," Cornford answered with deep feeling. "You won't get boxed up in this town—by anybody."

The train was close enough to the depot now for the sound of the locomotive's pistons to be heard. The three men started across the open area with its flag decorations. Behind them, the crowd had diminished: most of them convinced it was now too late to expect a further explosion of violence. But Hart and Burke were still there, fronting a knot of eager-faced men unwilling to admit disappointment until it was inevitable.

Steele, Zuckert and Cornford rounded the side of the depot building and there was just one man there. The liveryman, who was standing by the two geldings, two empty pails in one hand and the remains of a bale of hay under his other arm.

"I did like you asked, mister," he said anxiously.

"Grateful to you," Steele told him.

The liveryman hesitated. The shrill wail of the train whistle triggered him into movement and he scuttled away.

"The railroad man who runs the depot only takes care of shippin' out livestock," Zuckert said as he peered along the track to where the locomotive was slowing for the run in to the depot. "You buy your tickets from the train conductor."

The din of hissing steam, squealing brakes and rattling wheels precluded further talk for a while: the noise doubly as loud because there was a locomotive at either end of the six cars—the one at the rear coupled in reverse in preparation for hauling the train back along the single track spur to Friday Wells.

The two hitched horses tried to rear as the lead engine clanked to a halt a few feet from them, panicked by the noise and stench. The reins held fast. Gray steam hissed across the boarding and the evening breeze snatched at the dark wood smoke and drove it downward to further impair vision.

The engineers aboard each locomotive closed down their valves.

"Steele, you bastard!" Bob Porter yelled. His footfalls and those of other men thudded against the boarding as they came around the far side of the depot building.

The men who had come to watch suddenly whirled and scattered from the danger of back-stopping bullets which missed the intended target.

"He said he was a careful guy," Billy Cornford rasped.

Steele had glimpsed Zuckert pivoting and lunging for the cover of the building side. The smoke thinned and cleared. Porter came to an abrupt halt. Likewise Gus Young and Chuck Burton who flanked him. No sixguns were drawn, but eager hands hovered over butts. Startled faces were pressed against coach windows. Passengers who were about to descend from the train abruptly withdrew back aboard.

"Back off, kid!" the scowling Porter ordered. "Just me and the dude. Sixgun against his fancy rifle."

"You got a little too much sixgun," the young artist challenged.

"Only here to even things up if anyone figures to throw in with the dude," Gus Young said

59

coldly, locking stares with Cornford. "Me and Chuck the both."

Porter waited impatiently for the slow-talking Young to finish. His hooded eyes were fastened on Steele's unmoving features. "No one gets away with beatin' up on me," he warned. "And I figure my iron against yours will kinda round off the day right. Decide which of us is top man."

The Virginian gave an almost imperceptible nod. "You got nothing to lose but your life, feller."

"Damn it, Phil Fish won't like this!" Burke croaked from the safe cover of the depot building.

"Now!" Porter yelled, and went for his gun.

The Colt Hartford whipped down from Steele's shoulder.

Faces drew back from the car windows.

"Mine, Porter!" a new voice snarled.

"Enough!" Zuckert commanded.

It was the sheriff's Spencer that cracked out the first sound to puncture the instant of silence which followed the competing shouts. His bullet dug splinters of wood out of the boarding in the space between Porter's splayed feet. The tall gunslinger's revolver, the Virginian's rifle and a third gun exploded a split-second later, almost as a single sound.

But Porter's gun was pointed at the boarding in front of him as he fell forward, gushing two streams of bright crimson from a pair of holes close together in his chest. Even before Porter took the bullets in his heart, Young and Burton had drawn. Young snapped down into a crouch and swung his gun high, aiming at Zuckert who was standing on the roof of the depot building.

Burton pivoted toward the train, the muzzle of his Remington sweeping to locate the man who had claimed Steele and backed his demand with a bullet.

The Spencer spat lead in a puff of smoke and the man on the train fired a second shot. Zuckert's bullet smashed through the top of Young's skull and drove deep into his head. The hired gun was hurled over backward, his dying scream forcing a welter of blood from his gaping mouth. The man on the train scored a second hit to the heart and Burton continued to pivot another half turn before he dropped, colliding with the crumbling body of Young.

"Back in the holster, Fish!" Zuckert bellowed, training his Spencer on the platform of one of the cars.

There was a moment of tense silence, then the subdued sound of a revolver sliding into leather. But the aim of the lawman's rifle did not waver and he remained as rigid as a rock carving up on the roof. Boot leather scraped over the metal floor of the platform and then Phil Fish moved down on to the steps.

"I figure I put my shot into Porter before you did," he said to Steele.

He was younger than the Virginian and a couple of inches taller. But thinner to the point of looking emaciated. With a little more flesh on his colorless face, he might have been handsome. But his cheeks were too hollow, his eye sockets too deep and his bone structure too prominent. He had the round, staring eyes to match his name. His garb was all gray, from Stetson, down over neckerchief, shirt and pants to his spurred boots. The sole relief from his neutral color was the brass of the bullets slotted into his gunbelt and the white of the pearl handles on his matched Tranters.

As he spoke, he pushed off his hat and it hung down his back on the neckcord. His slightly pointed skull was totally bald.

Steele had started to slope the Colt Hartford to his shoulder when he heard one of the deadly Tranters going back into its holster. Thus, he faced Fish in the same manner as Porter a few moments earlier. "There was no money on it, feller," he said evenly. "So I don't reckon to argue the point."

"Back on the train, Fish!" Zuckert ordered. "Friday Wells has had its fill of gunfighters today."

Fish was ignoring the lawman with his eyes. "I don't much care where it happens," he told Steele, and then his cold eyes flicked their steady gaze to Cornford. "Be happy to kill the both of you any place."

The one-armed kid's grin was as carefree as ever. "We ain't worried."

"Get on board all of you!" Zuckert growled. "Let's get this train rollin' outta Friday Wells."

Fish gave a curt nod and turned to go back up the steps, banging into Jake Whitfield who was right behind him. Hart and Burke elbowed their way to the front of the knot of men who had emerged from cover when the heat went out of the situation. They glowered at Steele and Cornford and boarded the train at the point where Fish and Whitfield had gone from sight.

"What the hell, sheriff?" the engineer growled

62

as the Virginian and the artist unhitched their horses. "Railroad don't want your town's troubles pushed on to it!"

Zuckert spat as the leading arc of the sun touched the highest ridges in the west and turned the light as red as the drying blood which stained the three corpses. "Don't give me no argument, mister," he snarled. "Our mortician's got more work than he can handle right now."

The livestock car was at the rear of the train, which had become the front now that the end of the spur line had been reached. Because the bodies of the three gunslingers blocked the boarding, Steele and Cornford led their geldings around the locomotive and along the far side of the train.

A middle-aged woman in a large-brimmed hat was staring angrily out of an opened window. Her face was pale and she was breathing deeply of the cool evening air. She heard the two men approaching and swung her head to face them with a start. She gasped on recognizing Steele.

"Young man!" she snapped hoarsely. "That is the most disgraceful display of violence I have ever witnessed!"

"I thought you handled the rifle with a lot of grace," the grinning Cornford countered the criticism. "You got a real smooth style."·

The Virginian touched the brim of his hat as he led the gelding in front of the car window where the woman stood. "You keep sticking so close to me kid and you could cramp it," he muttered.

"I admire the best of everythin', Steele," the

artist said. "And you gotta know you're the best there is with a rifle."

The Virginian's horse began to lay a trail of fresh droppings and Steele glanced over his shoulder with a wry smile altering the line of his mouth. "If this was a bull," he told Cornford evenly. "That would have been your answer."

Chapter Four

The train pulled out of the Friday Wells depot as soon as the two horses had been loaded into the livestock car. Nobody else was riding out of town that night and none of the passengers had detrained at Friday Wells. There was a Negro in the car to take care of the livery duties and for fifty cents each from Steele and Cornford he agreed to unsaddle the two geldings and wax the leather.

The Virginian took his coat and rifle and the one-armed youngster carried just a sheaf of fresh drawing paper and a pocketful of charcoal sticks as they went through into the first passenger car.

The train was not crowded and this day car was less so than the others: for the passengers who had been in it had hurriedly left to find seats elsewhere when Fish and the three cowboys entered. It was an unfancy car, with pairs of padded seats facing each other along each side and an aisle down the center. Unlit lamps swung from the ceiling and there were watercolor paintings of Western scenes on the walls between the windows. Fish, Whitfield, Hart and Burke were at the far end of the car. The gunslinger sat alone on one side of the aisle while the other three were on the other side. Fish was in the process of lighting a long, slender cheroot as Steele and Cornford entered.

"Like you men to know somethin'," Fish said around the cheroot clamped between his teeth. "You won't be dying 'cause I been paid. Clif Reese got me out of a jam once and I owe him. These fellers ain't payin' me a cent."

He had to shout to make himself heard above the clatter of the wheels and the rumble of the locomotive. But it didn't seem to cause him any strain.

Steele dropped down into a seat just by the door, facing along the car. Cornford went swaying down the center aisle.

"Bad to lose that kinda friend," the youngster replied. "Means he can't be around to help you out of this jam."

There was still a little sun showing at the top of the western ridges. It shafted a dull red light through the train windows. Enough to illuminate Fish's face as the gunman clamped his lips around the cheroot before snatching it away from his mouth. And the pale face suddenly had a little color—a roundel of pink at the center of each cheek, dished in the depths of the sunken flesh. He recovered quickly and tried to conceal what he had felt by flashing a thin-lipped smile. But Steele had seen enough to know that Fish suffered from the same handicap as Porter: a possible fatal disadvantage for a gunfighter. He allowed himself to be needled into anger.

"It was girl trouble, *sonny*!" Fish said. "Pleasure. Business problems I always handle myself."

"So why do you bother with girls?" Cornford asked sardonically.

Fish was not too bright. He frowned as he tried to find an insult in the comment. But then he gave up. And the smile was back on his thin face as he swung on the seat and thrust out his legs across the aisle.

"Where'd you think you're goin', *sonny*?" he demanded, stabbing the cheroot back between his teeth.

"Make a few bucks," the artist replied as he halted short of the barring legs.

"You can't take it with you, they say."

"It's only you figures I'm goin'."

"You ain't countin' us, Cornford!" Jake Whitfield growled.

The kid looked over his shoulder and along the car at where Steele had resumed his seat after closing a window and putting on his sheepskin coat. "What do you reckon about these three, Steele? They count?"

The Virginian was pushing a fresh shell into the chamber after ejecting the spent casing. "Don't amount to much," he answered.

The door on the other side of Fish's legs was pushed open and the uniformed conductor entered the car. He was a short, plump, round-faced man of about fifty wearing wire-framed spectacles. He pulled up short and blinked at the scene which greeted him. For a moment, he seemed on the

67

point of turning and scuttling back the way he had come. But then he pulled himself up to the limit of his stature and resolved to treat the situation as though there was nothing wrong with it.

"Smoking's only allowed in the club car, sir," he said. He wore false dentures which added a whistle to his voice.

"Ain't no one complainin'," Fish answered, directing a cloud of smoke up at the conductor with the words.

The railroadman licked his lips and the glower he gave the gunfighter was totally lacking in force. He could not hold the cold-eyed stare and he glanced around desperately. "That so?" he inquired. He drew glares from the cowboys and nothing from Steele. He found Cornford the most engaging man in the car, and the artist grinned at him.

"It's all right, pops. Ain't no one gonna deny a condemned man his final smoke."

The patches of color showed on Fish's cheeks again, in the last ray of sunlight before the red orb slipped from view.

"*Sonny!*" Fish rasped. "I just don't know how you got to live so long with that bad mouth of yours."

"Please, gents!" the conductor said hurriedly. "I beg of you, no trouble on the train. Where d'you all wanna go? I got to write tickets for you. Regulations."

"Where's the next stop?" Fish wanted to know.

"Place you got on, sir. Perry Springs."

"Make it six for there," Fish said. "I'll treat."

Cornford looked over his shoulder at Steele again as the conductor produced a pad of ticket blanks and a pencil and began to write furiously. "He ain't all bad, Steele."

"Heart as big as Texas," the Virginian responded, reaching under his coat to bring out his newly acquired bankroll.

"You won't be able to miss a target that size."

"They say ambition's a fine thing," Fish countered, and this time he did not allow Cornford's barb to rile him.

"Feller," Steele called. "When you're through with those tickets, make out one from Perry Springs to Santa Fe."

Fish vented a harsh laugh. "That ain't just an ambition, dude!" he taunted. "That's a dream even bigger than Texas."

He swung his feet from across the aisle and rested them on the seat opposite him. The conductor ripped off filled out tickets and distributed five of them, accepting Fish's money with a nervous hand. Then he moved down the aisle of the rattling car, stopping three times to fire the wicks of the swaying lamps. Outside, as the two locomotives began to strain against the upgrade of the track curving out of the Friday Wells valley, twilight was losing the struggle against dusk and night hovered on the brink of descent.

Cornford moved to leave the car.

"Sure hope you ain't figurin' to try to run away from me, *sonny*," Fish said with heavy menace.

The young artist made a noisy sound of disgust in his throat. It was so uncharacteristic of Cornford, that Steele switched his attention from the ticket-writing conductor to the scene at the far end of the car.

69

"How many arms have I got, Fish?" Cornford demanded, his tone just short of a snarl.

Steele knew the kid had a short temper when the wrong circumstances were right. The only other time the Virginian had seen the fuse lit, Clifton Reese had taken a bullet in the brain.

Fish liked the fact that he had reached a tender spot under Cornford's skin. "I count only one, *sonny*," he said grinning around the cheroot. "But I don't make no allowances for cripples if they happen to be the hit."

"Used to have two," the artist rasped, and appeared to be trying to bring himself under control. But his voice retained its angry edge and his blue eyes glittered in the lamplight as he glared at Fish. "Lost the other one on account of I never run away from anything—or anyone."

The gunfighter's expression became even more arrogant in response to Cornford's bitter tones. "Okay, you sold me, *sonny*," he said as the conductor tore off the ticket and gave it to Steele in exchange for the fare. "You ain't all bad mouth."

The conductor was as apprehensive of Steele's lack of overt emotion as of Fish's aggressiveness. With Cornford gone, he found the atmosphere in the car oppressively hostile and he almost ran down the aisle.

"No trouble on the train gents, please!" he called as he stepped out on to the open platform.

The door slammed closed behind him and the clatter of the train's uphill progress diminished. Steele was grateful for the opportunity he had had, and taken, to rest in the lobby of the San Juan Hotel. The day had not been an arduous one, but the constant heat had wearied him and had he not enjoyed the period of relaxation, the motion and regular rhythm of the train's noise might have extended a soporific effect. And now was not the time to withdraw from sharp alertness.

Phil Fish intended to kill him and had a reputation to maintain. If it was inevitable, the thin gunfighter would certainly be ready to meet the Virginian in a showdown. No hired gun got to be worth a thousand dollars without proving such a value in front of independent witnesses. But such a man, by the very nature of the business he was in, would be unlikely to pass up the chance of an easy kill if it was presented to him.

So, as the pushed and pulled train reached the top of the grade and began to pick up speed across a wooded plateau, Steele did not allow his concentration to wander or to diminish for an instant. He sat erect in the seat, Colt Hartford resting across his thighs, coat collar turned up around his ears and hat tipped slightly forward to throw the top half of his face into shadow.

Down at the other end of the car, Fish was sitting sideways on his seat, leaning into the aisle while he listened to the low-voiced talk of the cowboys. He had crushed out the fire from his cheroot under a boot but the old smoke he had expelled clung to the car, its odor growing stale. Even though all the windows were tightly closed, the car became colder by the moment with draughts knifing in under the doors at each end. The heat of the day in Friday Wells was now pleasant to recollect as the mountain air attacked the unheated interior of the clattering train,

71

driven by the night wind which had grown out of the evening breeze.

Phil Fish had come prepared for the changeable weather of the Continental Divide's high country. He lifted down a valise from the rack above his seat and took out a coat which was wrapped around him from neck to calves when he draped it over his shoulders. It looked like an army greatcoat with plain buttons sewn on to replace the original insignia. The color was Union blue.

Whitfield, Burke and Hart shivered as the night air penetrated through their thin clothing.

The talk had ended now and Fish had adopted the same posture as Steele, matching the Virginian's steady stare from the cover of his hat brim's shadow. Whitfield, who was also sitting face-on to the length of the car, gazed disinterestedly out of the window. Burke and Hart leaned their heads back, perhaps staring up at the ceiling.

"You still got no objection to me smokin', dude?" Fish called suddenly, delving a hand under the long coat.

It was his left hand. Steele had already taken note that the ivory carving on the butt of the man's right Tranter was more worn by use than that on his other gun. And the hand went under the gun too high up for a draw, anyway. A cheroot was pulled from Fish's shirt pocket. Steele said nothing and the gunfighter lit the cheroot. He leaned forward to drop the match in front of it and step on the flame. His right hand went under his coat while he was in the seated stoop.

Lower this time. And he came upright like a whiplash.

Steele went sideways off his seat, swinging and cocking the rifle as he squatted into a crouch. For an instant, Fish continued to grin around the cheroot gripped between his teeth. But then his mouth fell open in a gasp. The heads of the three cowboys snapped around to stare along the car at Steele. The Colt Hartford exploded before anybody could duck.

The bullet smashed into the lamp which swung above and five feet in front of where the four men were sitting. The angle of the trajectory sent the slug up through the metal oil container and then into the glass shield before hitting the car roof. The gunfighter and the cowboys yelled in alarm and anger as shards of broken glass and licks of flaring oil rained down on them.

"What the friggin' hell?" Whitfield snarled, snatching off his hat and beating out the flames that were starting to get a hold on the felt.

The Virginian powered upright and rested the barrel of his rifle on top of the backrest of a seat. It was pointed off all the targets as the four men stood up and glared at him.

It was Fish who recovered first, both his hands in sight again, as he stooped quickly to retrieve the cheroot which was rolling from side to side in the aisle. He relit it from a small fire on the seat upholstery before putting out the flames with a boot.

"My fault," he acknowledged for the benefit of the angered cowboys. "Knew he could shoot that fancy rifle straight. Wanted to know how fast he was."

73

He dropped down onto his seat and swept his grin from Steele to the cowboys and back again.

"He ain't no slouch," Hart said tightly.

He and the other two resumed their seats, anxiously checking themselves and their surroundings for further traces of fire. The acrid smell of charring was strong in the cold, less well-lit atmosphere of the swaying car.

"What you might call a real hot shot," Fish agreed with a nod.

Steele was still standing, his loose-limbed body moving with the motion of the speeding train, when the door at the far end of the car burst open. Everyone looked at the grim-faced conductor who stood on the threshold, peering through his eyeglasses at the smashed lamp, the fire damage and then the men. An icy stream of air curled in around him and drove the smell of burnt fabric down toward Steele. The railroadman's uniform coat was open and the butt of a small caliber revolver showed in a shoulder rig.

He had entered angry, expressed fear in the face of the men, but then managed to summon up some courage.

"That's it!" he yelled, back-kicking the door closed and striding down the aisle. "You men have damaged railroad property! My job's to protect it. I'm gonna stop this train and put you off. Try and stop me if you want!"

He was already past the four men at the far end. And he looked everywhere but at Steele as he hurried toward the Virginian: moving without difficulty, like a man who had been born and bred aboard a speeding train.

"What we want is to get off!" Fish called after him. "You do your duty, man!"

Steele stepped aside to allow the conductor to pass him. Then he sat down and watched the door at the far end, expecting to see Billy Cornford enter the car. But the one-armed artist failed to show. Fish kept glancing at the same door. The trio of cowboys talked excitedly amongst themselves.

The lead locomotive engineer began to sound his whistle in a series of blasts. There was a distant acknowledgment from the man running the engine at the rear of the train. The note of the thudding pistons altered, the rhythm of the clattering car wheels slowed and then the brakes were applied. The highpitched squeal of friction became the dominant sound, imprinted strongly over the other sounds of the slowing train. Glowing sparks showered out from beneath the cars. Passengers from one end of the train to the other had to hold themselves in their seats or were thrust against them by natural force.

The train stopped, the locomotives hissing steam with an angry note: as if they were living things enraged by the interruption of their schedule. Fish looked out of the window on one side of the car while the cowboys checked the other.

"Over here," the gunfighter decided, jerking a thumb toward the window.

Steele glanced in that direction. A three-quarter moon shone down out of a cloudless sky, bathing its blue-tinged light over a rugged landscape of jagged rocks relieved here and there by the softer lines of timber stands. A carpet of white frost crystals glinted in reflection of the moon-glow.

"Too steep this side," Whitfield reported.

The door behind Steele opened and the conductor leaned in, his small .38 handgun drawn. Beyond him, the Negro was silhouetted in the open doorway of the livestock car. The whites of the black man's eyes were stark and staring against his flesh.

"All right, you men!" the conductor barked, the gun in his hand giving authority to his voice and stature. "Off the train and settle your differences where you can't do no damage to nothin' 'ceptin' yourselves!"

Fish was talking in low tones to the cowboys. All four of them appeared to be ignoring the railroadman. Then, as a group, they rose and the gunfighter led the way out of the car at the far end.

"You as well, mister!" the conductor growled at Steele. "Seems to me you're the main cause of this trouble."

The Virginian sighed as he stood up, sloping the rifle to his shoulder. As he stepped out on to the ground the conductor extended his free hand. His fingers opened from around a slender sheaf of bills.

"Refund on the Perry Springs to Santa Fe fare, mister. Seein' as how you won't be makin' the trip. Calvin is about to unload the mounts of you and your friend."

Steele took the money and pocketed it as he went down the steps. "Something I'd like you to know, feller."

"What's that?"

"Cornford's no friend of mine. Trouble just naturally follows me around. I don't encourage it by shaking its hand."

"Then that's your problem, mister," the conductor told him curtly. "I just got rid of all mine."

"Wouldn't count on that," the Virginian drawled, not looking back at the conductor as he ambled away from the train.

He kept his attention riveted on Phil Fish, who was already fifty feet from the track, having walked in a straight line at right angles from where he stepped down off the train. None of the cowboys were in sight. As Steele walked, his boots made crunching sounds against the thick coating of frost on the rocky ground. Behind him, shod hooves thudded hollowly on the wooden ramp as Calvin urged the reluctant geldings out of the shelter of the car into the biting cold of the night air.

Fish was not watching Steele. Instead, he was facing the train, the light from its windows shafting out at the base of a steep, brush-covered slope. Eager and anxious watchers were pressed against every window except in the first day car.

"You people!" Fish yelled. "You look good at what's gonna happen here. And you remember the name Phil Fish when you tell the story."

The horses were off the train and Calvin left them, their reins hanging down to hold them still.

"We ain't stoppin'," the conductor countered as the Negro started to raise the ramp. "Train's got a schedule to keep."

Fish took a final draw agaisnt his cheroot, then flicked it away to the side as Steele halted: ten yards distant from the gunfighter on a line parallel with the stalled train.

"Tell him, Jake!"

The conductor swung around as Whitfield's voice rasped from the footplate of the lead locomotive.

"Train stays where she is! On account me and Burke got our guns in the necks of the engineer and fireman."

"They ain't lyin'!" a frightened voice called.

"I'm gonna make a full report of—" the conductor started.

"Won't take but a minute!" Fish cut in, and continued to ignore Steele as he swung his head to look along the length of the train.

Hart stepped down from the platform of the rear car. "Phil, the kid turned yellow and beat it!" he called.

"Yellow ain't my color!" the familiar light-toned voice of Cornford countered. "I'm strictly a black and white man."

Only those who had stepped off the train were able to see the artist when his voice indicated his position. Steele, Fish, Hart, the conductor and Calvin peered at him: kneeling on the roof of the second car, stooped over a sheet of his stiff drawing paper. His single hand was already busy, sketching charcoal lines to start his picture.

But the watch on him lasted for less than two seconds. Then, as if some mechanical process had been started, Steele and Fish locked stares and the eyes of everybody else became fixed on the two.

"I ought to thank you, dude," Fish said softly as he raised his arms and hooked his curled fingers under the lapels of the long coat. "When word gets spread my sixgun took a rifleman like you in a fair showdown, I just got to be worth double what I am now."

He folded back the coat, shrugged his shoulders, and it fell to the ground behind him. He dropped his arms to his sides, slightly bent at the elbows so that his hand hovered level with the ivory butts of the matched Tranters.

"Happy for you, feller," the Virginian replied, as Fish turned slightly sideways on to him, narrowing the target. "But, like you said they say, you can't take it with you."

Cornford's charcoal screeched on the paper as the artist made haste to capture the scene. Hart's boots crunched frost as the shivering cowboy moved along the side of the train, not halting until he was equidistant from Fish and Steele.

"He'll call it," Fish instructed.

The Virginian experienced a coldness in the pit of his stomach that had nothing to do with the bite of the high country weather. He knew what caused it. Fear. It was a healthy sign because he had proved it to be part of his survival kit on more than one occasion: during and since the war. Men who found the word distasteful when applied to themselves preferred to call it respect for the enemy. But Steele acknowledged the naked emotion for what it was: aware that if a man did not experience fear in a dangerous situation he was a fool who increased his chances of dying.

Fish was a thousand-dollar hired gun who had not achieved his reputation with vocal bravado. And neither the killings at the Friday Wells depot nor the incident on the train had proved he was better with a gun than Steele or *vice versa*.

The Virginian saw the taut line of the gunfighter's mouth beneath the moon shadow of the man's hat brim and knew that Fish was also scared. He was aware that one of them would have to die to provide conclusive proof.

"Wait!" Billy Cornford called. "I ain't quite finished yet!"

The eyes of Steele and Fish remained locked together, as if linked by invisible, high-tensile wires. The wind, which had not been blowing since the train was halted, breathed a sudden, icy gust down the brush-covered slope. Steele's right thumb itched to cock the hammer of the Colt Hartford, but innate instinct forced him to resist the impulse. It was another advantage to Fish: added to his experience as a gunfighter. Despite everything the Virginian had become after the watershed in his life caused by war and the brutal slaying of his father, he could not escape the effects of his early upbringing. He still retained the inherent qualities of a southern gentleman: qualities that precluded any kind of cheating or double-dealing.

So his right hand remained as unmoving as every other muscle in his body as he faced a man who would try a double-cross at the least opportunity. But the opportunity did not present itself. And Billy Cornford supplied Steele with a life-saving opening.

"There you go, Fish!" the kid announced. "Not bad, uh?"

Fish could not resist accepting the implied invitation to look at Cornford. The lock which had held the two pairs of eyes was broken and the gunfighter glanced toward the artist on the car roof.

Steele did not. He watched and waited. Watched as Fish's posture stiffened and the man's mouth twisted into snarl of anger: and waited until his rigid body turned and the snarl found vocal outlet.

The gunfighter's hands swooped to grasp both Tranters. But only the one on the right came out of the holster. Steele's left arm swung across the front of his body, gloved hand cupped to accept the falling rifle barrel as his right wrist flicked, thumb hooking back the hammer. Fish's anger at what Cornford had shown him kept the man as stiff as a board. He was still fast enough for his draw to be blurred. But his action was a little mechanical: lacking smoothness. And his feet stayed planted hard on the frosted ground.

Tranter and Colt Hartford exploded simultaneously. But Steele swung his left leg to the side and leaned his body in that direction: holding the rifle steady. The .43 caliber bullet from the Tranter cracked his right upper arm. The Colt Hartford's .44 slug slammed into Fish's chest. Because the man was so flat-footed and rigid, the impact of the bullet did not send him into a stagger. He was forced into a half-turn as his right hand dropped low, releasing the Tranter. Death drained the anger from him and his legs folded.

He corkscrewed to the frozen ground and lay still.

"Dear God, this is crazy!" the conductor gasped.

Steele straightened and turned to glance at Hart, swinging the rifle in the wake of his gaze. "Little late with the call, feller," he said quietly into the tense silence which had preceded and followed the conductor's words.

The cowboy gulped. "Mister, he didn't say he was gonna pull nothin' like that, I swear it."

The Virginian shook his head as he started back toward the train, elevating the direction of his gaze as he shouldered the rifle. "Wasn't Fish who pulled anything."

Cornford was still kneeling on the roof, but he was no longer stooped over his work. He was holding up his finished drawing, grinning across the top of it. The moonlight showed clearly the black lines on the white background of the paper: a realistic portrayal of one man standing erect while another was sprawled on the ground in front of him. Even if the rifle had not been shown, Steele was obviously the man who survived. Cornford had accurately captured the lines of the Virginian's tense profile.

"Ain't always true what they say about art imitatin' life, Steele," the kid said. "Can be the other way around."

"With a little help from the artist," Steele answered.

Hart was still shivering and it was no longer entirely on account of the night air's coldness.

"Take off your gunbelt, feller," Steele told him.

As the cowboy hurried to comply, his fingers fumbling, the Virginian glanced at the conductor and the Negro. "Be grateful if you fellers would reload the horses."

The railroadmen nodded vigorously and started to do as they were asked. Whitfield and Burke climbed down from the locomotive, the former trying to conceal his nervousness with angry innocence. Both men had holstered the guns which had held the locomotive crew hostage.

"What's the big idea, dude?" Whitfield blustered. "You proved your point and we sure ain't gonna go up against you."

"Take off the gunbelts," Steele ordered softly. And now he permitted himself to cock the rifle sloped to his shoulder.

Burke followed the instruction at once. Whitfield glared at his two partners, then at Steele, and finally at the inert form of Phil Fish. He grimaced, looked sick, and unbuckled the gunbelt.

"What you gonna do?" he asked as the belt hit the ground.

Steele nodded to the nearest way up onto the train. "Get aboard. I'm making a citizen's arrest."

The trio halted as they were about to get on the train. "What charge?" Whitfield demanded.

"Holding up a train."

Cornford had clambered down from his perch and ambled over to stand beside Steele. "That oughta be worth a few bucks," he said eagerly.

"It weren't no holdup!" Burke whined. "Fish said to keep the train from rollin' so he could ride back to Perry Springs. We didn't take nothin' or hurt nobody."

83

"You hurt my damn feelings!" a man growled from the locomotive.

"And cost everyone some lost time," Steele added.

"He'll never make it stick," Whitfield insisted to his partners as the three of them stepped up onto the car platform.

Steele watched them flop down into seats, then turned his attention to the livestock car as Calvin and the conductor managed to herd the two geldings inside.

"I've still got my ticket to Santa Fe, feller," he told the conductor. "You want the money back?"

The elderly railroadman heaved up the ramp, with Calvin inside the car, and eyed the Virginian balefully through his eyeglasses. "I trust there will be no further trouble, sir," he said apprehensively.

"I'll take a ticket to Santa Fe, as well," Cornford put in brightly.

"In which case, I make no guarantees," Steele countered, pushing the sheaf of bills at the conductor as he swung up onto the day car platform.

The railroadman accepted the money, then ushered the kid aboard and hauled himself up. The engineer whistled the starting signal to the locomotive crew at the rear and the train moved sluggishly forward. Nobody looked at, or mentioned, the stiffening body of Phil Fish crumpled on the frozen ground.

In the car, where Steele sat across the aisle from the three cowboys, the conductor wrote a ticket for Cornford and then the young artist moved back down the train to earn some more money with his talent. The conductor ambled in his wake. Whitfield cleared his throat.

"Phil would have blasted you clear outta these mountains hadn't been for that crazy kid spookin' him, dude."

"I reckon," Steele agreed with a nod.

"It don't matter," Burke growled. "He didn't just kill Fish. He got his reputation to boot. Some fast gun somewhere who fancies his chances will blast the dude pretty soon."

"Hey, that's right!" Hart exclaimed.

Whitefield's glower became a grin. "Yeah! You get the picture, dude?"

The Virginian nodded again. "I get it, feller. Because I also happen to be in it."

Chapter Five

The train pulled into the adobe and frame town of Santa Fe as the first light of dawn was drawing the darkness from the eastern sky. A fine rain was falling, but the bitter cold of the high desert country night had diminished.

It wasn't much of a town, but it was the largest the train had stopped at on the long trip through the night, and the railroad company had its main office there, behind the depot on Main Street. The manager was standing under the office porch, sheltering from the rain, his glowering eyes switching from his watch to the noisy locomotive as the train squealed to a halt. Then he reached back into the doorway, grabbed a yellow slicker and hung it around his shoulders to dash through the rain and climb up onto the boarding.

"You're thirty minutes late!" he yelled up at the locomotive crew.

The train had only the one engine now, the other having been uncoupled at Perry Springs where the spur to Friday Wells started.

"Weren't their fault, Mr. Jansen," the conductor explained as he hurried to climb down onto the boarding and reach the shelter of the depot awning. "Had trouble with some passengers."

Santa Fe was the end of the line and, along the length of the train, passengers made haste to leave the cars: anxious to feel the solid ground beneath their feet after so many hours of being swayed and jolted by every motion of the clattering cars.

Jansen was a man in his late thirties. Tall and broad, but weak and soft because of his desk-bound job. When his anger was replaced by anxiety, every trace of character went out of his regular features.

"Trouble? What kind of trouble?"

"This kind, feller," Steele put in before the conductor could reply. He had stepped down from the first day car, Colt Hartford canted to his shoulder. A sideways jerk of his head encouraged Whitfield, Burke and Hart to follow him out into the rain.

Jansen eyed the passing passengers, his anxiety mounting as he saw the expressions of distress, disgust and irritation underlying their weariness. "Come inside!" he said suddenly, pushing open a door and stepping into the depot ticket office.

The conductor went in hard on the manager's heels.

"You heard the feller," Steele told his three charges.

As they entered the office, where the ticket seller was in process of stoking the fire in a pot-bellied stove, the conductor was already started on a fast-spoken account of the gunfight and holdup in the mountains. Steele leaned against the wall just inside the door and listened. When the story was finished, Jansen swept his gaze over the faces of the three miserable-looking cowboys and the nonchalant Virginian. The manager was still wearing his anxious frown.

"Any denials?" he asked after a long pause in which it seemed he did not know what to say.

"He told it the way it was, feller," Steele replied. "All I want to know from you is where I collect the reward for bringing in three hold-up men."

"We didn't take nothin'!" Whitfield defended.

"Sure didn't," the conductor said. "And it was him damaged railroad property. Shot out a car lamp and burned some seats."

Jansen looked as if he wished the conductor had kept quiet. He chose to ignore him. He shrugged, looking at Steele. "Company makes provision to offer rewards, mister," he allowed. "But there'll have to be an investigation. Folks'll have to be questioned. I reckon the sheriff ought to be informed. Law, anyway. Of some kind. I never had this problem before."

The Virginian nodded his approval. "I can wait for a while. Answer anybody's questions who has the right to ask. Leave the prisoners in your custody as senior company official. Be at the best hotel in town when I'm needed."

"Wait, I don't know. . . ."

Steele didn't hear any more of the anxious plea, for he had swung out of the office and closed the door behind him. Outside, the depot had emptied of passengers. The only man in the vicinity was Calvin. The Negro was standing in the rain beside the lowered ramp of the livestock car, holding the bridle of Steele's gelding.

"Grateful to you, feller," the Virginian told him, taking up the reins and swinging into the saddle. "Which is the best hotel in Santa Fe?"

"Take your pick, sir," Calvin answered, as nervous as everybody else. "Ain't one of 'em up to much. But if you got more money than any other folks, you get the best the hotel can give."

"Hey, Calvin!" the conductor yelled, sticking his head out from the ticket office doorway. "Run down to the law office and raise Sheriff Tucker. Tell him Mr. Jansen needs him here at the depot."

The Negro seemed happy with the chore: grateful to get away from the aura of menace that he sensed was emanating from the Virginian astride the gelding. Steele clucked to his horse and heeled him forward into an easy walk on the trail of the running Negro.

Dawn was fully broken now and the entire sky was a slick, slate-gray color with not a single break in the low cloud. The rain continued to fall, lightly but incessantly. And it had obviously been falling for a long time, because the broad street between the one and two story buildings was a static river of ankle-deep mud. There were no sidewalks at this end of town and the stragglers among the former passengers of the train were still struggling through the mire as the horseman rode by. Smoke was curling from many chimneys and the appetizing aromas of boiling coffee and frying food wafted out through many unshuttered windows.

Sheriff Tucker was unwilling to dirty his boots in the mud and he came around a corner astride a black mare. Calvin trotted behind the lawman, making a point of not looking at Steele. But Tucker looked long and hard at the Virginian as the two riders passed: either recognizing Steele from a description, or sensing that this man and trouble just naturally went together.

Steele continued on past the first hotel he reached, for there was a horse hitched to the rail outside. The animal was Billy Cornford's good-looking gelding. Half a block farther on was a building with a sign that proclaimed the doorway below was open to all men for all purposes: SANTA FE TRAIL'S END—HOTEL RESTAURANT SALOON CANTINA. LIVERY AT BACK. A token walkway of a single board rested on the mud between the hitching post and the door. There were a lot of muddy footprints on it. Steele pushed open the solid, one-piece wooden door and saw some of the people who had left the footprints.

The door gave directly on to the saloon-cantina section of the two story building. Three rain-sodden men stood at the bar, drinking whiskey, with their luggage on the sawdust-strewn floor beside them. At the far end of the bar, another man was in the process of registering. At the back of the room, three women were climbing wearily up the stairway, led by a fat Mexican burdened with their valises and carpetbags.

A slender, beautiful Mexican woman of about thirty sat at a table with a steaming cup of black coffee in front of her. She wore a plain black dress that clung to her firm curves and angles like a second skin. Her long hair and the pupils of her large eyes were as black as the dress. Her blemish-free skin was olive colored and the only make up she wore was the bright crimson paint on her full lips.

"Good morning, *señor!*" she greeted brightly. "What can the house of Rosabella Sierra offer to such a famous man?"

"It can take care of my horse and me, ma'am," Steele answered, touching the brim of his hat. "But you're mistaken. Famous I'm not."

Her teeth showed extremely white between her heavily painted lips as she smiled. "The Mona Lisa was not a famous lady on the first day she was painted, *señor.*" She indicated the elderly woman at the end of the bar who was taking care of the hotel register. "If you will check in, *Señor* Steele, I will have someone attend to your horse."

The Virginian nodded his acknowledgment, but did not go directly to the point she had indicated. Instead, he angled to where the three men were drinking at the bar.

"Mind if I take a look at that, feller?" he asked a portly, middle-aged man who looked like a drummer. He stabbed a gloved finger at a roll of stiff, white paper sticking from the man's topcoat pocket.

"Sure thing," the man said quickly, and took a hefty swig at his drink after handing over the paper.

Steele unrolled the paper and saw that Billy Cornford drew as well from memory as from immediate reality. The charcoal drawing was a quarter the size the artist usually worked with. It was a portrayal, with certain omissions, of the scene at the Friday Wells' depot just before the train pulled out. Steele was shown, with a smoking rifle, standing in front of the crumpling figures of Porter, Burton and Young. The train and depot building were shown, but Phil Fish and Sheriff Zuckert did not appear in the picture. The drawing was unsigned, but it had a boldly-lettered title: THE DUDE HANDS OUT FRONTIER JUSTICE TO THREE GUNFIGHTERS.

"The kid's pretty good, ain't he?" the drummer said with a nervous smile. "And he's got reasonable prices. Picture only cost me fifty cents."

"This one, too."

"And this."

The drummer's drinking companions had taken rolls of stiff paper from their bags. They held them up for Steele to see. One was a copy of the scene Cornford had drawn at the train's unscheduled mountain stop. The other showed the Virginian standing beside two horses with bodies slumped over the saddles. They were respectively entitled: PHIL FISH MEETS HIS MATCH WITH THE DUDE and THEY TRIED TO ROB THE DUDE.

"He's a real artist," Steele agreed wryly. "In more ways than one."

"At settin' his prices right," the eldest of the trio said as he rolled up his drawing. "You don't have to charge high if you can do the volume. And that youngster sold to near everyone on the train."

"The *señor* wishes a drink?" the Mexican bartender asked.

"Coffee and some breakfast after I've cleaned up," Steele told him as he moved along the bar to register.

As he signed the book, the fat Mexican came down the stairs and grimaced as his beautiful boss shot a burst of Spanish at him. Then Rosebella Sierra switched to her attractively accented English. "Meals are served here in the cantina, *señor*," she said as the fat man waddled reluctantly to the door and went out to attend to the horse. "I will have the cook prepare something for you."

Steele gave her a smile and a nod as he accepted a room key and started up the stairs. He recalled what the Negro had said about the Santa Fe hotels and realized it was not only his new-won reputation as a gunfighter which had preceded him into town. The downstairs, adobe-built section of the hotel was large, but spartan, and not particularly clean. His second-floor room at the front was small, spartan—and not clean either. Nevertheless, he was obviously going to get the best available because news of his financial success in the shooting match had also been spread.

From the dusty window he looked down into a street that was empty again: and up at a sky that was still dropping rain but which showed signs of brightening in the east. Then he took off his hat, sheepskin coat and jacket and stretched out on the bed. Five minutes later, after raindrops had ceased to tap gently against the window, heavy footfalls sounded on the landing outside. He called for his visitor to come in after the knock sounded.

"I think perhaps you need these, *señor*," the fat

Mexican said as he opened the door. He was only in his twenties, but in bad shape. He breathed deeply after the exertion of unsaddling the gelding and carrying the saddle-bags and bedroll up the stairway.

"Grateful to you," Steele told him. "Dump them somewhere and then get some hot shaving water for me, uh?"

The overfed, high-colored face showed a grimace. But then an avaricious grin suddenly transformed the set of the features. Steele had reached into the pocket of his jacket hanging over the back of a chair. And he held up a fan of five one-dollar bills.

"One of these is for the trouble," the Virginian told him. "Other four are for the use of your ears."

The small eyes blinked several times. "Benito's ears, *señor*? They are fixed to his head. I don't think he—"

"Use them, feller," Steele cut in. "If you hear any talk about the name Steele or the dude, you come to me and tell me what is said. All right?"

The grin, which had faded suddenly, appeared again. Benito nodded enthusiastically. "*Sí, señor*. Benito can do that."

He advanced across the room, took the offered money, and withdrew fast: like a hungry animal capturing its prey. Steele caught the odor of cooking food rising up the stairway just before the door closed. Benito did not take long to fetch a pitcher of steaming water. Steele took his time cleaning off the dirt of the train ride, and shaving.

Like his inability to cheat at anything and his

94

taste for stylishly cut clothes, Steele's almost fastidious penchant for personal cleanliness was another relic of the distant past of his rich youth in Virginia. After he had cleaned himself up, he brushed off his suit before leaving the room. He carried the rifle with him. The sun had broken through the cloud and the first sweat of the day opened his pores as he went down the stairs.

The elderly woman had gone, taking the register with her. The three men were still drinking at the bar. There was a knife, fork and condiment set on the table where Rosabella had been sitting. Benito was waiting at the foot of the stairs.

"You are to sit at the table of *Señorita* Sierra," the fat man said expansively, leading the way in the manner of a big city major-domo. His gestures were flamboyant as he held Steele's chair. He leaned close to whisper as Steele sat down. "Those at bar talk only of what lousy town is Santa Fe, *señor*. Do not think much business to be done here."

"You're doing a good job," the Virginian complimented.

Benito moved away hurriedly as a door at one end of the bar swung open and Rosabella swept regally out, carrying a heavily laden tray. The drummers interrupted their discussion to follow the woman with avid eyes. She had the grace and elegance to match her looks, swaying her hips and holding her body in a carriage of subtly underplayed sensuality. Benito and the bartender had seen it all before and were indifferent to the woman.

"You do not object to eating breakfast with

me, *Señor* Steele?" she asked as she set down the tray.

There was steak and grits and fresh-baked bread for the guest. The apparent owner of the place had just another cup of coffee, which she poured from a pot after Steele had raised himself from his chair and waved her into the seat opposite.

"You have a special reason for coming to Santa Fe?" she asked, pouring coffee for Steele.

"It's as far as the train went," he answered. The steak tasted greasy, but it was tender.

"And you hope to collect money for the three men you brought to office of railroad company?"

Steele showed a quiet smile in response to her bright one. "News sure gets around fast in this town."

Rosabella shrugged and her conical breasts rose and fell engagingly under the tight fit of the dress bodice. "Santa Fe is a small place in the middle of a big nowhere. Little that is worth talking about happens here. News from outside is eagerly awaited and well used."

Steele glanced around the saloon. "Your place, ma'am?"

"Since a year ago, when my husband was killed. He was American, like you. From the east, where I think you come from, too." Sadness entered her dark eyes. "But he was not like you in any other way. He was a man of peace."

"You said killed. Not died."

"He was out visiting a friend. The horse bolted and the buggy overturned. It was cruel and tragic, but such things happen in life." She shrugged again, and worked the smile back on her lovely face. "Without misfortune, one would not be able to fully appreciate the good parts of life."

Steele did not respond as he continued to eat his breakfast. The three women who had registered ahead of Steele came down the stairs, but were not served by Rosabella after they had chosen a table. It was Benito who took their order for breakfast and went through into the kitchen. The drummers, having lined their bellies with liquor, felt able to tackle the storekeepers of Santa Fe. When they went out, they left the door open. The noise of a fully awake town came in with the shaft of bright sunlight. Jansen, the railroad company manager in Santa Fe, and Sheriff Tucker entered a few moments later.

They made straight for the table shared by the Virginian and Rosabella.

"Like to talk to this gent, Mrs. Moffatt," Tucker said flatly. He was a tall, rangy man in his mid-forties with a face that was as ragged and stained by life as his clothing was by wear. The whites of his eyes were veined from drinking or lack of sleep. He had a slack, weak-looking mouth.

The woman eyed him with ill-feeling as she stood up. "I have told you many times, *señor*, Miss or *Señorita* Sierra. I am no longer married."

Tucker ignored her as he took the chair she had been using. He eyed Steele with the same brand of ill-feeling Rosabella had expressed toward him. "How much was you figurin' on gettin' for bringin' in those three cowpunchers, mister?" he asked.

Jansen already had a hand in his jacket and he

wasn't the kind of man who carried a gun. Steele finished chewing the final piece of steak, put down his knife and fork and swallowed some coffee.

"Whatever the going rate," he answered evenly.

Tucker pursed his loose lips. "There ain't one for this kinda thing. I been talkin' to folks and it seems this wasn't your ordinary train holdup. Mr. Jansen here don't want to press charges on behalf of the railroad company. And the engineer and his fireman are content with the apologies they got."

"So everyone's happy but me," Steele commented without rancor.

The lawman toughened his tone. "Mr. Jansen is prepared to overlook the matter of damaged railroad property. And, since the shootin' happened outside my jurisdiction, I sure ain't gonna do nothin' about that end."

"But you went to the trouble of bringing in the three men," Jansen said, a little impatiently. He withdrew his hand and dropped an envelope on the table. "So I propose to refund the fare from Perry Springs to Santa Fe."

"Advise you to accept the offer and let things rest that way," Tucker urged.

"You hear me complaining, feller?" Steele asked, picking up the envelope and transferring it to his pocket.

Jansen felt sufficiently relieved to show an infrequent smile. Then he experienced the need for a drink to settle his nerves. Tucker remained seated.

"You're not the kind of man who uses words to

say what he's thinkin', mister. You let that there rifle do it for you. Keep it quiet while you're in Santa Fe."

The warning drew nothing from Steele and the lawman stood up. He moved to the door, then had to back off as three men turned in off the street. Because of the dazzling sunlight behind them, he didn't recognize the men until they were inside. Whitfield, Burke and Hart strolled arrogantly to the bar, feelings shared between scorn for Steele and lustful admiration for the statuesque Rosabella. Tucker carried a single holstered Remington on his gunbelt. He draped a long-fingered hand over the butt.

"I got a peaceful town here!" he barked, commanding the attention of everyone in the saloon. "But there's a big jailhouse if it's needed." The bloodshot eyes swung between the three cowboys and Steele, leaving no doubt about who were being warned. "And there's a gallows right out back of it."

"Quit that talk, sheriff!" Billy Cornford said to break the seconds of tense silence that followed the threat. The one-armed artist stepped into the saloon. He was wearing the familiar grin and carrying the tools of this trade under his arm. He nodded toward the cowboys. "You're makin' them guys nervous."

"Aimin' to scare them clear outta my town," Tucker growled, and grimaced toward the Virginian. "Him, too."

Cornford shook his head. "Not until he's ready to leave, sheriff. He's got nerves of Steele." He laughed. "That's his name."

Tucker's grimace cut deeper lines into his ill-used face. "I'll remember it, in the event I have to hang him."

"Kindly leave my place, *señor!*" Rosabella snapped. "Your talk is making everybody nervous."

"You worried, Steele?" Cornford called as he headed for the bar and Tucker turned to leave.

The Virginian pursed his lips. "No, feller. No part of my plan to be highly strung."

Chapter Six

It was a quiet morning in Santa Fe. But only those buried in the town cemetery passed it more peacefully than Adam Steele. For he slept until one o'clock in the hot and dusty room on the second floor, the window closed against the everyday sounds of the town's routine. Under a sky which had become cobalt blue in the wake of the departing clouds, there were comings and goings at the Department of New Mexico army headquarters; the town's businessmen bought and sold supplies; and everybody else with a job went about his or her chores. Traffic from surrounding farms and homesteads rolled on streets which had been baked by the hot sun from muddy mires into strips of rock hardness. The noon stage had arrived on time and left thirty minutes later with a fresh driver, shotgun and team. It had delivered six passengers to Santa Fe. Ten had left—all of them from the train which had rolled into the depot at dawn.

Two of the newcomers were youngsters. Marcus Seward was a fresh-faced kid of seventeen with blond hair and clear blue eyes. Myron Nolan was four years older. He had dark, brooding eyes in a pock-marked face and wore a thick black mustache that drooped around each corner of his mouth.

Both of them had, independent of the other, asked questions concerning the whereabouts of the man called "the dude." And both had started drinking in the Trail's End Saloon less than fifteen minutes after getting off the stage in Santa Fe. Benito, who had never had as much as five dollars in his pocket at one time in his life before, applied himself well to the job he had been given: and heard about the questions the youngsters were asking.

"Señor!" he hissed as Steele stepped from his room at a few minutes past one o'clock. Ever since Seward and Nolan entered the saloon, the fat Mexican had been positioned at the top of the stairs—from where he was able to watch the youngsters and the room door. "I have news for you. Bad, I think."

Steele leaned the Colt Hartford against the wall and started to pull on his black gloves as Benito came toward him. "Tell me, feller. I promise not to cry."

The comment confused the Mexican for a moment. Then he launched into a fast, low-voiced description of the two youngsters. Then: "The younger one, *señor*. He drinks whisky too much. The other, he sips the beer. Only two he has had. Both wear the two guns. Good-looking guns."

"Grateful to you, feller," the Virginian

102

drawled, canting the rifle to his shoulder. "Keep looking and listening, uh?"

"*Sí, señor!*"

The fat Mexican turned and hurried along the landing and down the stairway. Rosabella Sierra, who was eating lunch at her table, yelled at Benito: demanding to know where he had been loafing. Then she cut across his lying explanation to demand he go into the kitchen.

Steele moved to the top of the stairs and surveyed the saloon, wrinkling his nostrils against the mixed odors of liquor, cooking and body sweat. He saw Rosabella. Then Whitfield, Burke and Hart who were playing cards at a table. The three ladies he had seen at breakfast were now eating lunch. Billy Cornford was doing a sketch of Jansen. There were a dozen other customers in the saloon, all men. A mixture of Mexicans and Americans. Either drinking at the bar or eating at tables. He had no difficulty in picking out Seward and Nolan from the descriptions Benito had given him.

He started down the stairway into the saloon where the atmosphere was heavy with smoke layers and heat; and noisy with the buzz of conversation and sounds of eating and drinking.

"*Señor* Steele!" the beautiful owner of the place cried happily. "We will eat together again, no?"

Her words immediately curtailed the noise and it was apparent that she alone was not aware of the latent menace which had crouched in the sun-bright room. For, while everyone else expressed taut expectancy, the woman showed puzzlement.

"Seems like a nice idea," Steele answered softly as he reached the foot of the stairway and started across to the table where Rosabella sat.

"Bartender, give me another drink!" Marcus Seward demanded, banging his empty shot glass on the bar top.

Like the younger man, Myron Nolan had also swung around sharply and looked at the Virginian as his name was called. Now he turned his back. He sipped his beer. From outside came the thud of running footfalls against the baked mud of the street. The sound diminished as the man in a hurry ran away from the Trail's End.

Steele's boots sounded very loud on the sawdust-strewn floor.

"Goodness, it really is not!" one of the three ladies said, and nervousness gave her voice a hoarse tone.

"Deal the cards, Jake," Burke rasped.

A lot of other talk started, voices cancelling themselves out into blurred mumbles. Steele reached the table, hung his hat over the back of a chair and sat down, resting the rifle across his thighs.

"What can I get for you, *señor?*" Rosabella asked, her usual brightness marred by her still-present reaction to the tension.

"Whatever you're having, ma'am."

"It is Mexican."

Steele nodded. "When in New Mexico, do like the New Mexicans."

She looked at him hard, but learned nothing from his neutral expression. She rose and moved gracefully toward the door which led into the kitchen.

Seward accepted the closing of the door as his own prearranged signal. His final whiskey had been sunk and he banged down the glass. The bartender moved toward him, but pulled up short when the youngster whirled around.

"Okay, dude!" Seward snarled.

His words brought back the silence. It hovered in the hot air, seemingly with as much physical presence as the layers of blue tobacco smoke.

"You talking to me, kid?" Steele asked.

His voice was just a moment behind the screech of Billy Cornford's charcoal in entering the silence.

"On your feet!" Seward barked. His face was very red and his lower lip was moist and trembled a little. But his strong-looking hands were rock steady as they were held in claws, each an inch from the butt of a holstered Frontier Colt. Six feet from where he stood, the back of Myron Nolan became a little hunched. Nolan was the only customer who did not flicker his attention back and forth across the fifteen feet of space separating Seward and the Virginian.

"Always eat sitting down," Steele answered.

"How about dying?" Seward's voice was as controlled as his hands, despite the quivering lower lip.

"Like to do that lying down, kid. In bed and old if I have my way."

Seward shook his head, unblinking blue eyes fixed in a direct stare on Steele's face. "You lost your chance of that when you got yourself a rep, mister. Now, I'll kill you sittin' down if that's the way it has to be. Anyone want to call it?"

"Be a pleasure!" Jake Whitfield answered enthusiastically.

"Whatever is the world coming to?" one of the trio of ladies exclaimed. There was excitement in her voice.

"To an end for the dude!" Seward snapped. "Call it mister. Count of three is fair to all concerned."

Steele had his gloved hands resting on the table top. He raised his left leg slightly. The Colt Hartford tilted and slid. The stock hit the floor first, then the rifle measured its length on the sawdust.

"Get up and pick it up!" Seward ordered, his confidence boosted by what he assumed was a sign of nerves in the Virginian.

It sounded clearly in his voice and caused Nolan to glance over his shoulder. His pock-marked face expressed a nagging anxiety. But then he realized it didn't matter one way or the other. If Seward killed the dude, then he would make his play against Seward. It was not important from whom he inherited the reputation.

Steele swung his legs from under the table and stayed on the chair, facing Seward, as he leaned forward and down. There was one aspect of the Virginian's clothing which never altered, whether his appearance was freshly turned-out or the worse for wear. Always, the outer seam of his right pants leg was split along the length of the calf. And, when his leg was bent, as now, the split gaped. But the wooden handle of the throwing knife with the six inch blade was never visible through the opening.

The Virginian reached out his left hand slowly toward the frame of the Colt Hartford. He kept his eyes fixed upon Seward and saw the kid was concentrating on the left hand. Then the blur of movement as his right hand went into action caused an instant of panicked confusion in Seward's mind. During that instant, as running footfalls thudded against the hard street again, Steele's hand delved into the split seam. His gloved fingers curled around the handle of the knife and he drew the weapon from the boot sheath.

He powered upright and forward from the chair. The rifle stayed on the floor. Rosabella came out of the kitchen, screamed and dropped the tray of food. Nobody looked at her. Steele used the impetus of his rising to send the knife spinning through the air. From seeing Seward drinking, he knew the kid was right-handed. And it was the revolver on his right side that was gripped first. The gun stayed in the holster.

The knife dug deep into the fleshy part of Seward's right forearm. The speed and power of the throw swung the arm back against the front of the bar. When the arm stopped moving, the knife kept on going. The scream of the injured kid masked the thud of the blade's point sinking into the wood of the bar front. Seward half-turned and swung his left hand across the front of his body to grip the vibrating wooden handle of the knife. Blood squeezed between the flesh and metal at the entry and exit wounds and dripped to the floor, soaking into the sawdust.

Everyone—including Nolan—stared at the screaming Seward, who could not bring himself to yank out the knife from his own flesh.

"What's goin' on here!" Sheriff Tucker roared

107

as he pulled up short in the open doorway, his gun drawn.

The black face of Calvin peered into the saloon over the lawman's shoulder. Both were breathless from a fast sprint.

"Watch out!" Jake Whitfield yelled.

He had been the first to look away from Seward: and seen Steele following up the knife throw. The movement off the chair had led to a fast, long-strided, silent run. But not toward Seward. It was Nolan who found the Virginian closing on him as he whirled. Tucker roared a curse and exploded his sixgun. The bullet cracked over the heads of Nolan and Steele and showered dust motes and wood splinters from the ceiling. As Nolan went for both his guns, his expression caught between a snarl of anger and the lines of fear, Steele's hands were already positioned for the attack. His right fastened around Nolan's left wrist. And his left streaked away from under the lapel of his suit jacket. Nobody saw what was in it until the hand came down hard and open over the back of Nolan's right hand. As Seward's expression of pain subsided to tearful sobs, Nolan screamed.

The ornate head of a tiepin was clutched between Steele's middle fingers. As Nolan sagged against the bar and the Virginian stepped back from the youngster, the metal of the pin was withdrawn from the wound it had pierced through the hand. It had gone in through the back and burst clear at the base of the palm. Its entire length was sheened with crimson blood. Like Seward, Nolan brought his good hand across to wrap around the injured one.

"You sneaky bastard!" Nolan screamed, dropping down into a crouch and holding both hands against his belly.

"Be grateful, both of you!" Steele said tautly.

Tucker cursed again and lunged into the saloon, his gun wavering across the three combatants.

"You could be dead," the Virginian augmented, and leaned toward Seward.

"Steele!" Tucker warned.

But Steele ignored him. Seward jerked his good hand from the knife before Steele could knock it away.

"Vicious sonofabitch!" Hart growled as the Virginian reclaimed his knife.

His expression showed no spite, but his action was completely without mercy. He raised his knee, pressed it against Seward's wrist, gripped the knife handle, and yanked the blade from the flesh and the wood behind it.

"Steele!" Tucker said again, blustering now.

The Virginian merely glanced at him, then at the two youngsters. He decided that, even had Seward and Nolan been fit enough to try for retaliation, the lawman was covering them.

"You're sure remembering my name pretty well, sheriff," he said, his voice back to its normal drawling tone.

"Nobody has to know your name, mister!" Nolan snarled as Steele returned to his table and sat down. "Just the dude is good enough. 'Cause you look just like in the pictures."

Steele took a napkin from the glass in the center of the table and started to wipe the blood from the knife and the tiepin.

"Cut out all this damn back and forth talk!" Tucker roared. "And someone tell me what's goin' on here!"

Benito had emerged from the kitchen following Rosabella's scream and the crash of the falling tray. Since Seward and Nolan had been disabled, the beautiful woman and the fat man had been whispering frantically at one another. Now Rosabella raised her voice and spoke in English.

"I will tell you, sheriff!" She pointed at the injured youngsters. "Those two came to Santa Fe on the noon stage. They asked questions about the whereabouts of *Señor* Steele. They find out he is staying at my place. They come here and they start trouble. I demand they be arrested for disturbing my guests."

It was obvious Tucker didn't enjoy being on the receiving end of an order from the beautiful woman. His glower did not alter as he swept his gaze from the two men to the woman.

"I want them out of my place!" Rosabella insisted. "That blood they are dripping is spoiling the appetite of my guests."

Another curse hovered on the lawman's lips, but he held it back. "All right!" he snapped at Seward and Nolan. "Down to my office and answer some questions." He backed to the door, so that he was able to keep the youngsters in sight as well as the Virginian. "You, too, mister."

Steele had put away the cleaned weapons and replaced the Colt Hartford across his thighs. He turned to look over his shoulder, narrowing his eyes against the brightness of the sun shafting through the door behind the lawman. "My appe-

110

tite's still as good as ever, feller," he said softly. "I'll be down to the law office after lunch."

"Now!" Tucker yelled, swinging the gun to concentrate its aim on Steele.

"No more!" a woman wailed. "I cannot stand any more violence."

She was one of the trio of ladies eating lunch. As she spoke, she rose and knocked over her chair. She ran up the stairway. The other two followed her, casting frequent backward glances across the saloon.

"Pull the trigger or back off, feller," Steele told the sheriff. "I plan to eat, unless you reckon to shoot me in the back."

He turned away from the sheriff and nodded to Rosabella. The woman snapped a short sentence at Benito, who hurried into the kitchen as she swayed elegantly across to join Steele.

"It is to be hoped, *Señor* Tucker," she said distinctly, "that when you attempt to shoot a man in the back, your aim does not waver."

She met Tucker's enraged gaze with ice-cold defiance as she looked across the Virginian's shoulder.

"I hope it friggin' chokes you, you tough-talkin' bastard!" the lawman roared, then glared at Seward and Nolan and jerked with his gun for them to move.

"What's the problem between you and that feller?" Steele asked, as the two injured youngsters complied with the order to leave. He spoke softly, but his voice carried to every ear in the quiet saloon.

Rosabella's voice spoke out a lot louder. "When my husband died, the sheriff thought I would not

111

know the difference between sympathy and passion." A cruel smile altered the line of her full mouth. "It was painful for him to discover his mistake."

Seward and Nolan had reached the threshold of the saloon. Thus, Tucker was able to retreat from the bitterness of the woman and the leers and looks of disgust which were directed toward him from elsewhere in the saloon. When there were no longer human forms in the doorway to interrupt the angled rays of early afternoon sunlight, the cadence of normal saloon sounds resumed.

Benito delivered Steele's lunch with a conspiratorial wink. The trio of ladies returned to their table, two of them disappointed that they had missed the end of the excitement. Whitfield, Burke and Hart lost interest in the card game and called for drinks. Jansen paid Cornford for the sketch of himself and left to return to work. The artist gathered together his materials and trailed the railroad company manager to the door. But he halted beside the table where the Virginian and Rosabella sat.

"You've got hidden talents, Steele," he complimented, the familiar broad grin decorating his youthful face.

Steele sighed. "But you've got plans to unveil them from coast to coast, I reckon."

Cornford bent his head and used his teeth to draw one of his sketches from under his arm. He straightened to display the picture. It showed Steele, half-crouched at the side of the chair and about to hurl the knife at a poised Marcus Seward. The title was: COOL STEELE USES COLD STEEL. The artist skillfully released his teeth

112

grip on the picture and caught it under his arm.

"You're makin' me a fortune, you know that!" Cornford exclaimed happily.

"I also know what you're making me, feller," the Virginian drawled.

"But you can handle it."

"And when I can't, you're around to help me out."

The artist nodded, as happy as ever. "You bet."

"Not on you," Steele told him. "You're too much of an outsider to be anything but a loser."

The kid's grin turned a little sour and he hovered on the brink of anger. But then he gave a lopsided shrug and headed for the door. "Let's wait until the race is over, Steele," he called back.

Rosabella looked at Steele in bewilderment as the Virginian resumed eating. "I did not understand any of that, *señor*," she said.

"Something I don't understand, ma'am."

"What is that?"

"You're no gold-diggin chippy working in somebody else's place. So you're not after any more money that what I'm paying for room and board. But you are—"

Rosabella interrupted him, her eyes and voice becoming sultry. "The sheriff was the first man to approach me after my husband was killed, *señor*. Even had I enjoyed his company, it was too soon after the tragedy. But now the tragedy is old and much of the pain has gone. And I enjoy your company."

She was old and experienced enough to ignore the use of coyness. Her eyes as they met Steele's in a level gaze made a tacit but frank promise to deliver what she spoke of. During the brief period

113

that their eyes were locked, the sounds of the saloon receded from their consciousness. It was almost as if they were alone in the entire world.

But then a shout abruptly shattered the bubble of false privacy.

"Hey, everybody! Frank Gorman's comin' to town to get the dude!" The thick accents of Calvin's voice were easily recognizable.

Steele saw the concern cloud Rosabella's eyes, then quickly spread to depress her entire face. "Gorman isn't like the two Tucker just took out of here, uh?"

The woman caught her breath. "It is said he is the fastest man with a gun in all the southwest, *señor*."

The Virginian looked around and saw that he was once more the center of attention. "Benito!"

"*Sí, señor?*" The fat Mexican responded.

"Go up and pack my gear. Then saddle my horse."

Steele carried on eating as the crestfallen fat man went to do his bidding.

"Well, what do you know about that?" Jake Whitfield growled.

"He's takin' it on the lam," Burke taunted.

"That streak down his back is yellower than the noonday sun!" Hart added.

It was impossible to put a reason to the disappointment displayed on Rosabella Sierra's lovely face—whether because Steele was running from a gunfighter or running out on her.

"Sit tight, ma'am," the Virginian put in just before she could speak. He pushed back his chair and rose, putting on his hat and canting the rifle to his shoulder.

"Where are you going, *señor*?" she asked softly.

"To lose my reputation," he told her, loud enough for all to hear. But then he leaned close to whisper to her, catching the perfume in her coal black hair. "But I'll be back—and we'll work on losing yours."

Chapter Seven

Steele did not allow himself to vent his feelings
until he was alone in the hills west of Santa Fe.
Then, the emotions which had been broiling in
the pit of his stomach since he listened to the
taunts and insults while he rode from town, were
let out. They showed visually on his face, the features of which were contorted and colored by a
release of temper. At the same time, the unhear-
ing hills were assaulted by a snarling string of
obscenities which ripped from his gaping lips.

But the display of anger was short-lived as he
heeled the gelding into a flat-out gallop along a
narrow gully. And, when he reined his mount to a
snorting halt, he found he was sweating as heavily as his horse: and their breathing rate was a
match.

The manner of his leaving Santa Fe was in
direct contrast to his character. Never before had
he run away from the threat of personal attack.
Not even in the War between the States. Then,

there had been orderly retreat from superior Union forces, but on such occasions personalities had not been a factor.

From Santa Fe, he had ridden alone under the merciless light of the sun: his apparent cowardice plainly seen by anyone who chose to watch. And the entire town, with the exception of Rosabella Sierra, had chosen to watch him. The majority in silence. A few voicing the scorn which all felt. Jake Whitfield was the most vocal, augmented by Burke and Hart. Seward and Nolan snarled their contempt from cell windows in the jailhouse. Sheriff Tucker and Billy Cornford were among those who remained silent. But their eyes were strangely more expressive than words could ever be.

Steele said nothing and looked nobody directly in the eye. He stared straight ahead, discerning the occasional familiar voice against the chorus of taunts: recognizing a face here and there on the periphery of his vision. That was when his insides began to seethe and every muscle in his body had to be stilled from reaction by a physical effort. And, even when the town was behind him and the voices had faded from earshot, his anger continued to mount.

But he held it in check for a full thirty minutes. After that, he was out of sight of Santa Fe: and he gave way to the luxury of violent temper. Then reason prevailed and he brought himself under control. He stroked the neck of the gelding with a gloved hand and allowed the animal to make his own walking pace. His feet rested easily in the stirrups and he used only the reins—to veer his mount this way and that to ensure he stayed on ground that retained sign of his passing.

The switch to relaxed riding cooled both his body and mind and soon, as the afternoon drew close to evening, he was able to smile in recollection of his outburst. But not for long. The fact that he had needed to vent a reaction to his humiliation in Santa Fe was a bad sign. He had been able to keep it inside of him for long enough this time. But there could be another time in the future when there was no opportunity—or perhaps even no ability—to delay.

And Adam Steele would be as dead and stiff as Phil Fish up in the high border country between the territories of Colorado and New Mexico. Perhaps that time in the future was not far off, if Frank Gorman was as good as his reputation.

The sun was down behind the Divide and dusk was retreating under the attack of full night when the Virginian reached the top of a long, gentle slope and saw the derelict fort. It stood, desolate and sad, at the center of a broad and long plateau: no longer able to command the rugged terrain surrounding it. For its adobe walls had crumbled and the buildings behind them were nothing more than roofless shells.

As he rode closer, Steele saw that the blackness which scarred large areas of the sun-bleached adobe was not moon shadow: rather the searing marks left by a raging fire that had been largely responsible for the fort's ruin. But not entirely. In wresting the territory of New Mexico from its original possessors, artillery shots had blasted at this defensive position and rifle bullets had pitted its once proud walls.

The gates had long since rotted to a black wood pulp which had dried to a brittle state and crackled under the gelding's hooves as Steele rode through the gap in the fallen walls. The rain of the night before had been collected in every hollow and he allowed his horse to roam and drink at will after unsaddling him. Then he gathered wood which had once formed part of the fort's structure and lit a fire under the single remaining wall of the blockhouse.

The flames served a double purpose: to heat coffee and to act as a beacon in the event the man trailing him lost the signs he had left. When the gelding had drunk his fill, and foraged sufficiently on the tufts of coarse grass which sprouted among the rubble, the Virginian ground-hobbled the animal. Then he stripped, cleaned and oiled the Colt Hartford. After that, as the night sky grew overcast and the temperature dropped, there was nothing to do except feed kindling to the fire and drink coffee.

Sleep was not possible, for he knew his judgment was not infallible. He may have misread the situation and it could be that the man trailing him was not the one he expected. All he was certain of was that someone was on his trail—he had seen him, a small speck upon a slightly larger speck in the far distance, before dusk had foreshortened the horizon.

But staying awake during the three hours it took for his follower to catch up with him served no purpose. Steele saw nor heard anything until the man stepped around the wall and into the fringe glow of the fire. His voice announced his presence and the Virginian looked at the gun in

119

the man's hand before moving his impassive gaze up to the face. The Colt Hartford lay on the hard ground, firelight gleaming dully on the freshly oiled surfaces of the barrel, frame and cylinder.

"You don't surprise me, Steele," Billy Cornford said softly, the grave lines of his face suggesting he never smiled. "That you aren't surprised. You left a trail a five-year-old could follow. And the fire." He stepped up closer to the fire and squatted within range of its warmth. His sixgun stayed aimed at the Virginian. "And you're a long way from a fool."

"You aren't, feller," Steele told him. "I should have remembered you can move like a mountain lion when you need to." He smiled. "Or maybe it was just I didn't reckon you needed to."

The one-armed youngster didn't respond to the smile. "You have to hate me, Steele,"

The Virginian shook his head and poured himself a fresh mug of coffee. "Resent is the word I'd use, feller. You reckoned you saved my life outside the hotel in Friday Wells. And maybe you did. Which means I owe you something. I've never owed anybody anything before and I don't like the feeling of being in debt."

"I don't consider I'm owed," Cornford said. "And I sure didn't engineer that ruckus in Friday Wells."

"But you sure made use of it."

Cornford licked his lips. "You wanna know why? I got a good reason."

"Reckon I know why," Steele drawled, and sipped at the scalding coffee.

Cornford dropped into a sitting position, crossing his legs. The gun did not waver in its aim. "I've already allowed you're no fool."

"You turn up at a town in the middle of nowhere on a day when there's a shooting match. Then you stick close to me while I build up a reputation I don't want—helping me to get it and then making sure folks all over know I've got it." He sipped more coffee. "Seems to me you're looking for a fast gun, feller. And, when he didn't show up for the shooting match, you spotted a way to flush him out into the open. Gorman the one?"

The kid grimaced. "Gorman's part of the right name. But Frank ain't. It's Ed Gorman I want. Frank's pa." Then he smiled, but the expression lacked its usual humor. The blue eyes above the white teeth showed evil triumph. "But Frank Gorman has to die to flush out his pa."

"Ed took your arm off, uh?"

Hatred became the dominant expression in the kid's eyes. "Three years ago, in Springfield, Missouri. Ed Gorman led a gang against the First National Bank there. I worked in the grocery store next to the bank. When they came outta the bank, I heaved over a cracker barrel. Gorman tripped on it." A fleeting, wan smile. "Just a kid tryin' to be a hero. But Gorman didn't care how old I was. He just got to his feet and pumped a bullet to me. He was too mad to shoot straight. Hit me in the right arm. Bad enough, though. Wound got the poison in it and they had to cut off my arm."

Neither his face nor his tone invited sympathy. He was merely relating the facts of an incident that had happened to him a long time ago. But

Steele experienced an affinity with Cornford. Stronger than the rapport which had built up over the past two days. He had good reason to understand the bitterness of thirst for revenge.

"It didn't bother me much at first," the kid went on. "Well, not too much, anyway. I had this talent for art and I had been right handed. But I learned to draw again, with my left. Then I started to find out there's a lot of things in life a guy needs both hands for. And all the damn pityin' looks folks kept givin' me started to get on my nerves. So I learned to shoot as well as I can draw and then I made up my mind to make Gorman pay for what he done to me."

Steele showed a quiet smile. "But it didn't work out for you—single-handed?"

Cornford didn't grin at the humor. But neither did he react to the *double entendre*. "I did some research first. Found out the Gorman gang were still holdin' up banks and stages and trains, then goin' into hidin'. Found out, too, that Ed Gorman only gave a damn for two things—money and his son. And that Frank was out here in the southwest, buildin' up a rep as a gunfighter."

"So you tried to compete for his title, uh?"

A deep sigh. "Made a mistake. Who'd go up against a cripple in a showdown, Steele? I bet even a guy like Phil Fish wouldn't have faced me if he'd blasted you." The lopsided shrug. "The shootin' match was my last resort, until I heard Fish was comin' gunnin' for you. Then I got the idea."

Steele nodded. "Good one for you, feller," he allowed. "Bad one for me. I'm out in this part of the country because I've got a couple of murder charges against me back East. And I'm guilty. I don't want a reputation for anything. Especially an illustrated reputation."

The artist was not contrite. "Figured a man like you for somethin' like that, Steele. But there ain't nothin' I can do about it now. Things are rollin' and there's no way of stoppin' them."

The Virginian finished his coffee. "You reckon Frank Gorman will bother with a feller who ran from his reputation?" He leaned his back against the wall. "If he comes."

"He'll be here," Cornford replied, a little sadly. "I talked to Seward and Nolan while the doc was patchin' up their wounds. The folks who got off the train between Friday Wells and Santa Fe did a good job of spreadin' the word about you. Showed my drawin's all over. And Seward and Nolan both heard that Gorman knows you killed Phil Fish. They told Calvin."

"And what about me running, feller?"

The artist sighed. Then shrugged. "Ain't no way you can make me feel bad. But folks figure us for friends. When I told them you left town to keep from bein' hung after you've shot Gorman, they believed me. Told them you told me to tell them that."

He thrust the gun out at arm's length, expecting a violent reaction from Steele. But the Virginian did not move a muscle. He remained in an attitude of careful listening, but his ears were now attuned to a sound which came from much farther away than the kid at the side of the fire.

"And I guess you left even plainer sign than I did, uh?"

Cornford heard the sound then: the distant thunder of many horses galloping toward the derelict fort from the rugged terrain in the east.

"I'm almost out of drawin' paper. Tore up so much of it to mark the trail." His voice suddenly took on a tone of pleading. "Just one more time, Steele. With Frank Gorman dead, his pa is sure to come out into the open."

"And you'll take care of him?"

A vigorous nod. "Yeah. He's mine."

"Not a fast gun?"

An even more vigorous shake of the head. "Just a mean one, Steele."

The sound of the hoofbeats rose in volume as the riders neared the fort, galloping up the final slope to the plateau.

"And what about all the other Sewards and Nolans, feller?" the Virginian drawled. "The gunslingers who reckon they could have topped Frank Gorman so make a try for me—if I just happen to top him myself?"

Cornford blinked his perplexity and there was a moment, as his mind wandered to contemplate the future, when Steele could have lunged for his rifle and perhaps get the drop on the one-armed kid. But then the group of riders crested the rise to make the potential attempt pointless.

"Steele!" Cornford gasped. "I swear I never thought beyond gettin' to Ed Gorman." He slid the gun smoothly back into its holster before the newcomers could see he had been keeping the Virginian covered. But it took him longer to lose the expression of shock from his youthful face. "As God is my witness!" he added.

Steele eyed the men as they slowed their horses on entering the ruined fort. "This isn't your trial feller," he muttered. "I'm the one who could be going into the box."

Chapter Eight

Frank Gorman was in his mid-twenties and looked like he earned a good living from his reputation as a fast gun. He was dressed Western style, but his boots, pants, shirt, hat, topcoat and gunbelt were all brand new and of high quality. His build was big but owed nothing to excess fat. He had an angular face with an unblemished skin tanned darkly by sun. His eyes were slate-gray and clear and he looked well-fed and well-rested. There was a quality of cool confidence about him as he dismounted from his big, black stallion. Not overconfidence. He didn't smile as he watched the Virginian rise to his feet on the other side of the fire. Instead, his gaze rose and fell over Steele's slight form: surveying the opposition and estimating its threat.

"I got no hard feelings about you dragging me out here, mister," he said. "I don't want no hassle with the Santa Fe law after I've killed you."

He put his hands on his hips, parting his un-

126

buttoned topcoat. The gesture displayed the single sixgun he wore in a holster tied down to his right hip. An unfancy Colt. Then he looked at Cornford.

"You the one who draws the pictures?"

The youngster was looking hard at Gorman. Perhaps trying to see a family resemblance to the father. Or perhaps relishing the fact that he was just a generation away from his objective. He nodded.

"Then go get your pencil and paper, kid. But this time it'll be the dude who'll be a heap on the ground."

Gorman still was not overconfident. Just using the Virginian's own ploy of trying to unsettle his opponent by needling him. Steele ignored both Gorman and Cornford, as the latter shot a pleading look at him before hurrying away to where he had left his horse. Instead, Steele's dark eyes surveyed the retinue which had followed Gorman out to the fort. There were a score of them, Americans vastly outnumbering Mexicans. Whitfield, Burke and Hart had come. So had Seward, with his arm in a sling, and Nolan with a bandaged hand. Calvin was there. So was Jansen, trying to stay inconspicuous at the rear of the crowd.

"I don't know none of them," Gorman growled. "But I didn't make no objection to them coming. A man's reputation don't mean nothing unless it's seen he keeps it fair and square."

Steele pursed his lips and knew he had to go through with the gunfight against the beefy Gorman. Even if Cornford admitted the truth of the story Steele could tell, it would sound as if the Virginian was trying for an easy out. His apparent cowardice in leaving Santa Fe would be seen as proven fact. And, as a professional gun-fighter who considered himself the best, Gorman could not afford to walk away. The reason Phil Fish had been killed did not matter. Fish had been a fast gun and Steele had beaten him. Gor-man had to find out how much faster was the Virginian.

"Leave it!" Gorman snapped as Steele stooped to pick up the Colt Hartford.

A gun came out, but it wasn't Gorman's. It was Seward's left-hand side Frontier Colt. Steele froze for a moment in the stoop, then slowly straightened.

The spectators had dispersed from a group and had formed a line across the fort's compound. The firelight showed them clearly, and illumi-nated the length of open space in front of them. Seward aimed his gun from the center of the line, across the space and through the flames at Steele.

"My weapon is the sixgun, mister," Gorman said evenly. "And I don't go up against no rifle in a showdown."

Steele nodded. "Haven't carried a sixgun since Appomattox earned a place in history," he said.

The slate-gray eyes studied him coolly for a stretched second. Then the man gave a nod of his own. "I'm prepared to believe that. So I'll handi-cap myself. No call, mister. And I won't make my move until you go for your gun. How's that suit?"

"Could be the one I'm buried in," Steele replied softly, shrugging off his sheepskin coat.

Gorman showed a fleeting smile of satisfaction as he removed his own topcoat—and carefully

128

folded it before putting it on the ground. "Where's the guy who said he'd loan the dude a gun?" he demanded, stepping out from the side of the fire.

"There you go, dude!" Myron Nolan called. He had already unfastened the ties holding the holsters to his legs. Now he unbuckled his gunbelt one-handed and tossed it at Steele as the Virginian moved away from the other side of the fire.

"Where's the picture-man?" Gorman yelled, backing off until there was a gap of thirty feet between himself and where Steele was donning the gunbelt.

"Right here!" Cornford answered, appearing from behind the fire to squat beside it. He spread a sheaf of paper on the ground and held his pencil of charcoal at the ready.

Steele glanced at him and thought that the grin the youngster wore had a quality of craftiness about it. But he allowed it could have been the way that the flickering firelight caused shadows to move on the youthful face.

"Be careful of that kid, Gorman!" Jake Whitfield warned. "He spooked Phil Fish."

"I ain't so easy to catch as Fish!" Gorman growled, not breaking his concentration upon Steele. "Anytime you like, dude," he invited as Seward holstered his gun.

Steele had been looking down at the matching revolvers on his hips, not enjoying the discomfort of the unfamiliar gunbelt around his waist. "Something I need to do first," he answered, bringing up his head slowly to look across the firelit thirty feet.

"Sounds like he's shit scared!" Hart growled.

129

"No tricks, dude!" Gorman snarled.

"Never do fire a gun in earnest unless I've tried it for feel and pull, feller."

The lurking menace drained out of Gorman's stance and expression.

"Sounds fair to me," Calvin commented.

"Hey, don't let him fool you, Mr. Gorman!" Nolan countered, a little nervously. "He draws that gun, he'll start practicing on you, man!"

Gorman ignored the warning and used a finger of his left hand to inscribe a circle in the air. "Go ahead, dude. But just turn around and face the other way before you draw."

"Don't do it, Gorman!" Nolan yelled, his voice quivering with fear now.

Everyone detected it and attention was constantly switched between Nolan and Steele as the latter turned slowly and, just as slowly, eased the gun from the right hand holster.

"Sounds to me," the Virginian said, raising the gun, "that he agreed early on to loan me his revolvers."

There was utter silence in the fort. Even the fire ceased to crackle as Steele squeezed the trigger. The click of the firing pin hitting an expended shell sounded as loud as if a bullet had been exploded from the muzzle.

"No!" Nolan shrieked, and whirled.

Steele turned as slowly as before, raising his arm to aim the gun at the sky. He cocked it and squeezed the trigger. Cocked it and squeezed. Again and again until every chamber was proved to contain an expended shell case. But the proof was seen only by the enraged Gorman, who stared relentlessly at the raised gun. Nobody heard the series of clicks, for the the sounds were covered by those made by Nolan as the young gunfighter scrambled up the rubble that had once been a solid wall.

With fluid speed, Gorman suddenly turned, crouched, drew his Colt and fired. Nolan had reached the top of the rubble, his panicked form clearly silhouetted against the overcast sky. No one saw where the bullet took him. But it was instantly fatal, killing Nolan before he could utter a cry: and tossing his dead body over onto the other side of the rubble.

Gorman holstered his gun and drew himself erect before turning to face Steele. Every line of his face expressed earnest sincerity. "I believed you, Steele," he said. "I ask you to have the same kind of trust in me. I knew nothing about that lousy trick."

Steele nodded, accepting the other man's word. Then he hurled the gun in an underarm throw, arcing it into the center of the fire.

"Señor!"

More than twenty men had followed Gorman to the fort. One more. He must have stayed in the background a long time, for the Virginian could not have failed to spot the overweight Mexican. Now Benito stepped out from behind the rubble of a former fort building and moved forward. He was holding out a Dance Brothers .44, gripping it by the barrel. The kind of six-shot, single-action revolver Steele had carried as a Cavalry Lieutenant for the Confederacy.

"See what I buy with the five dollars you give to me, *señor*," the Mexican said. When he was close to Steele, he dropped his voice to a whisper

131

only the Virginian could hear. "*Señorita* Sierra sends me to see what happens to you."

"Grateful to you, feller," Steele responded for all to hear.

Benito backed away to assume the space in the line vacated by Nolan. And Steele turned his back on Gorman again, gloved hand wrapped around the smooth butt plates of the old gun. He aimed at nothing and squeezed the trigger. The bullet ricocheted off a piece of twisted and rusted iron. The gun had a hefty recoil and pulled slightly to the left. He slid it into the holster before he turned to face the waiting Gorman.

"Everything all right now?" the pro gunfighter asked.

His voice was thick as he shifted his feet to move sideways on to Steele. It wasn't fear, the Virginian knew. Gorman was still suffering from the effects of the injury to his pride. There was just his own word that he had not engineered the gun with the empty cartridge cases. On such un-supported evidence—and the added fact that he had killed the man who might have been his partner—there was a great deal of room for doubt. No, Gorman was not afraid of Steele. But he was unsettled by the circumstances.

"Fine," Steele called softly.

"Whenever you're ready."

The fire crackled. Cornford shifted his posture slightly and the fire's noise was angrier for a moment, as sparks were carried high in the black smoke. Then the charcoal screeched on the paper. The watchers held their collective breath, all eyes focused upon Steele as the man invited to make the first move. The Virginian had adopted the

132

same pose as Gorman, sideways on and with his right hand hovering close to the butt of the holstered revolver.

Stretched seconds passed. Steele stared at Gorman's face. Gorman's gaze was lower, concentrated on Steele's gun hand. Steele experienced the coldness in the pit of his stomach again. And he realized why Billy Cornford's initial plan had failed. The young artist had got him into this situation: of facing a man he did not know and might possibly like if he did know him; of having to kill this man or be killed by him. Cornford was the one who deserved a bullet from Steele yet, because he was just a kid with only one arm, the Virginian could not respond to the impulse to turn and kill him.

The fire exploded.

Gorman's eyes flicked to the right.

Cornford yelled in alarm and dived from under a shower of sparks.

The watchers gasped.

Gorman drew his Colt.

The Dance Brothers gun was part of a second later in clearing the holster.

But Gorman was looking and aiming at the fire. He had been no part of the war. Or, if he had, he never fought in a full scale battle with distracting sounds on every side of him: sounds that had to be ignored. Small arms fire. The pounding of mortars. The thumping of artillery. The screams of the dying. The pleas of the terribly wounded. If a man paid attention to such sounds in the heat of battle, he was in immediate danger of adding his own agonized cries to the nightmare of sound.

So Steele looked, aimed and fired at the man who had made the mistake. And Gorman took the bullet in his chest as he tried to rectify the error. He turned and fired, but Steele's bullet was already lodged deep in his heart. His shot went high as he staggered backward and started to crumple. His gun slipped from his dead hand as he hit the ground and lay still.

"What in heaven's name caused that to happen?" Jansen exclaimed, the first man to break the silence which followed the double reports of the two revolver shots.

Everyone had swung their attention away from the inert form of Gorman to stare at the now quiet fire. They saw, but ignored, the one-armed artist as Cornford attempted to rescue his sketch of the gunfight. The flames beat him and the drawing curled and crumbled to brown ash.

"Guess that gun of Nolan's still had some powder in the shells," Seward suggested.

"But it does not matter," a nonpartisan member of the audience said. "All saw the gun go into the fire. It was a fair contest."

"There is no disputing that," Jansen agreed.

The group looked at each other and heads bobbed in nods of agreement. Some, albeit, grudgingly. Then, as Steele unbuckled the gunbelt and dropped it to the ground while retaining a grip of the Dance Brothers revolver, all but one of the spectators moved to where their horses were waiting. The exception was Benito, who started forward, but then halted abruptly as Steele moved in on Cornford. The Virginian jerked a gloved thumb toward the heap that was Gorman's dead body.

"You going to kill his pa with your bare hand, feller?" he asked.

The hoofbeats of the men riding out of the fort barred anyone else but Cornford from hearing what Steele said. And *vice versa*. The artist followed the direction of the Virginian's gaze and looked down at his empty holster. Then he met the other man's level stare.

"It don't make no difference," he argued. "It was still a fair fight. Neither you nor Gorman saw me toss the gun in the flames."

The kid was right, and he had read the circumstances right. He had known the ice-cold Steele would ignore the sudden noise while the unsettled Gorman would be distracted by it.

"It's getting to be a habit," Steele said as the hoofbeats diminished into the distance.

"What?" Cornford asked.

"You putting my life on the line and then doing something to save it."

The kid nodded. "Bad habit, Steele. And I'm kickin' it as of now. I'll take care of Ed Gorman, just like I said I would."

"And all the trigger-happy gunslingers who come after me?"

Cornford showed a happy grin. "I figure you'll think of somethin', Steele," he said.

"*Señor?*" Benito asked apologetically. "I can have my gun back now?"

Steele turned to the fat Mexican and smiled. "It's a good one, feller."

"You maybe have a message for the *Señorita* Sierra?"

The Virginian pursed his lips as he held out the

gun toward Benito, butt forward. "Sure thing, feller. Tell her I'll be around to spend some time with her. But first there's one more iron in the fire."

Chapter Nine

Ed Gorman caught up with his son's killer a week
and a half later. Steele and Billy Cornford were
in the barren midsection of New Mexico Territory, on the trail between Alburquerque and Fort
Craig a few miles south of the Rio San Jose
crossing.

The first week after the showdown at the aban-
doned fort had been a bad one. Every trace of the
usual good humor had drained out of the one-
armed artist and he was irritable, constantly
complaining about the fact that the Virginian re-
fused to remain in one place for the elder Gorman to find him.

And Steele was edgy, minute by minute expecting Gorman, or a trigger-happy gunslinger, to appear. In the first instance to blast him without
warning and in the second to call him for yet another showdown.

But nobody approached the oddly assorted pair
until they reached Alburquerque. They arrived at

137

the tiny town shortly after the stage from Santa Fe: and Steele was buying supplies while Cornford purchased a replacement gun, when one of the stage passengers entered the store.

"You just gotta be the dude and the artist," he said from the doorway.

The newcomer showed a tight grin of satisfaction as the two men whirled. The man in the door was in his mid-forties and very fat. There was a gunbelt around his bulky waist, but the holster was empty.

"No trouble in my place!" the nervous storekeeper pleaded, his voice high-pitched.

"I found trouble, but I don't aim to start none," the fat man said, his expression becoming abruptly grave.

"Gorman's man?" Steele answered, successfully concealing self-annoyance at the way he had started.

"Right, mister. One of many. And I just earned myself fifty bucks for locatin' you. You plannin' to hang around this jerk-water town?"

"So you can get a message to Gorman?" Steele asked.

"What do you think, mister?"

"Tell you what I know, feller," the Virginian drawled. "I know I'll be moving south again soon as I've finished my purchases."

The smile almost came back, but adopted the lines of a sneer. "Makin' a run for the border? Won't help you none."

Steele shook his head. "Too hot to run anywhere, feller. I'll be riding easy."

Gorman's man stared long and hard at Steele. "All right." He swung out the doorway.

The Virginian and the artist left town without seeing him again. The one-armed youngster was more grouchy than ever, claiming it would have been better to wait in Alburquerque and end the matter quickly.

"There are two matters to be ended, feller," Steele told him coldly. "And I reckon they'll both be tied up more neatly where there aren't any witnesses to spread any more words."

Cornford sulked for a while, but finally acknowledged the truth of what Steele had said. Certainly when applied to his own business. The Virginian had given no clue as to how he planned to take care of shedding his unwanted reputation as a fast gun. And, as the days and the small settlements passed and the Virginian kept the promise of an easy pace, the artist's temperament improved. At the same rate, Steele's taciturn attitude became less irritable and assumed its normal nonchalance.

He was indifferent to his companion but not to his surroundings. Ed Gorman had made his intentions known but, if Cornford's researches were based on solid fact, the revenge bent holdup man was unlikely to remain so open. His method of robbery was to hit, run and hide. And there was no reason to expect he would alter his tactics in the pursuit of Steele.

It was late afternoon and still hot from a sun that had dodged the puffs of insubstantial white cloud all day. Steele was ahead of Cornford, the two of them holding their geldings to an easy walk in the shade of a high, steep mesa. To the east the ground fell away gently, barren and almost featureless into the broad valley of the Rio

San Jose. South—ahead of the riders—lay a narrow gap between the mesa wall and a tower of rock.

The rifle shot rang out as Steele led the way into the gap. The bullet was aimed high, ricocheting off the tower and slamming into the face of the mesa. Rock splinters were exploded from each point of impact.

"It's him!" Cornford yelled, jerking his new gun from its holster as he leapt from the saddle of his nervous mount.

"Don't reckon so," Steele answered evenly, reining his horse to a halt and stroking the animal's neck with a gloved hand.

Beyond the gap, the ground fell away sharply, the army trail to Fort Craig following the curve of the mesa wall to plunge into a gully. Two men with four horses stood in the gully, both pointing Winchesters. One of the rifles was smoking from the muzzle.

"He's right!" a voice called from above, as Steele made a narrow-eyed survey of the terrain: looking for the riders of the two spare horses. "But it won't be long before Mr. Gorman gets here."

The still-mounted Steele and the artist on the ground both stared up at where the lip of the mesa met the sky. The missing two men were up there: standing on the very edge of the cliff and aiming rifles down.

"Drop the gun, kid!" one of them ordered. "And you, dude, ditch the rifle."

Steele's stare was a short one, his eyes cracked almost closed to avoid the bright blueness of the sky impairing his vision when he looked away.

140

When he turned slightly in the saddle, clamping a hand around the frame of the booted Colt Hartford, Cornford was blinking rapidly.

"Do it and we're dead," the Virginian rasped, his lips hardly moving. "Soon as this rifle comes clear, start shooting."

"Where?" the kid asked, soft but desperate.

"Hurry it up!" a man down at the gully mouth demanded.

"Any damn where!" Steele rasped. "You won't hit them with that. But maybe you'll scare them a little."

He eased a foot out of a stirrup as he spoke. Then he started to draw the rifle slowly from the boot.

"Ditch the sixgun, kid!" a man on the mesa top snarled, and pumped a bullet down the cliff. Dust puffed eighteen inches from Cornford's right foot. The kid's horse snorted and lunged into a bolt. The animal just managed to squeeze between Steele's mount and the rock tower. A cloud of dust rose from under its thudding hooves.

"Damn!" a man on the mesa yelled.

"What the—!" came the start of a demand from the gully mouth.

Steele snapped the rifle from the boot, cocked it and flung the stock to his shoulder as he swung from the saddle. Cornford's Remington cracked. The Virginian's gelding reared and plunged into a bolt as its rider came clear. Steele squeezed the rifle trigger while he was still in mid-air. Rising dust clogged his nostrils and strung his eyes. It also toned down the brilliant blueness of the sun-bright sky.

Cornford got off a second shot. And he did hit

something: the plummeting body of the man who had taken Steele's bullet in the face. The body thudded to the ground between where Steele and Cornford were crouching. But the rifle which had slid from the dead hands struck the kid a painful blow on the curve of his back.

The men down at the gully snapped off two shots. But the angle at the top of the rise obscured the target. Off his horse and crouching, Steele was obscured by the crest of the rise. The bullets smashed into rock, showering more chippings down through the settling dust.

After his yell of pain, Cornford scrambled to snatch up the discarded Winchester.

"Cover the top!" Steele yelled against a backing of two more exploding rifle shots.

Cornford sat down hard on his rump and fired up at the lip of the mesa. A rifle barrel that had started to tilt over the edge was abruptly withdrawn. Steele tipped forward and crawled around the steadily firing artist and then rose into a half-crouch to skirt the tower of rock. On the far side, he was hidden from the man on the mesa. He inched forward, pressing himself flat against the rock. Gunfire continued to explode, allowing not a split-second of silence. He reached a position where he could look down the sloping trail. The geldings he and Cornford had been riding were gone. But the rearing and snorting mounts of the ambushers were held fast by tethers. Clear of the lashing and plunging hooves, the two men were squatting in the open and sending a hail of rifle fire toward the gap. There was a carton of fresh shells lying on its side between them, its contents spilled into the dust.

As one of the men stopped firing and reached for the heap of shells, the Virginian swung away from the warm face of the rock. He shot the still-firing man in the side of the neck and he half-rose, throwing his arms high and wide as he screamed. The gush of escaping blood arced from the punctured flesh and splashed across the hand grasping the bullets.

The owner of this hand did not waste time looking for where the killing shot came from. As his partner slammed to the ground, he powered erect and turned. He was two strides short of the cover of the gully when Steele's bullet drove into his back. The impetus of his run and the impact of the bullet pitched him forward, out of sight, but dead. A trail of blood-spattered, discarded bullets pointed the way to his resting place.

Steele didn't look at the pointer. Instead, he whirled and raced back around the tower of rock. Just before he re-entered the gap, Cornford cursed. His fire was curtailed for a stretched second. Then the less powerful crack of the Remington sounded. A Winchester replied from high above. Steele skidded to a halt, the Colt Hartford already elevated. He squeezed the trigger. The man above had been willing to risk showing himself against revolver fire. The reappearance of Steele took him by surprise. He had no time to withdraw this time. The .44 slug went in under his chin, up through his head and exploded in a welter of blood and bone splinters through the top of his skull. He was in a kneeling posture. He released his rifle and it clattered down the cliff face. Cornford leapt clear of it with a yell. Then the man's torso became limp and folded forward. It swung through mid-air and its weight dragged his legs off the edge of the cliff. He came down head first. There was the crack of his neck breaking as he hit the ground. Then the squelch of exploding flesh.

Steele ducked back behind the rock tower. Cornford caught some of the sprayed gore flung outward by the shattered body. But the kid showed no revulsion when Steele stepped out from cover and saw him using a neckerchief to wipe away the crimson stains. The fresh face was set in a bright grin.

"Damn it!" he exclaimed in high excitement. "Outnumbered two to one and yet we took the bastards!"

"Numbers didn't matter," Steele responded evenly as he ejected the expended shells from the rifle's chambers and replaced them with fresh ones. "We had all the advantage."

"How d'you make that out?" Cornford wanted to know, his glee unabated.

"Gorman wants me alive," the Virginian replied. "Why else the warning shots and not killing ones?"

"Hey, that's right!" the kid agreed. "But they'd sure have been happy enough to kill us after we made our move."

"Made use of our advantage by then," the Virginian said, canting the rifle to his shoulder.

Cornford nodded enthusiastically. "Did that, sure enough. What now?"

He scooped up his Remington, then sat down and held it between his knees as he reloaded it.

144

"You get what you want, feller. We stay here and wait for Ed Gorman."

"You sure this place is quiet enough for you?" the grinning Cornford asked.

Steele shifted his wry gaze from the two dead men in the gap to those down at the mouth of the gully. "It is now."

"Quiet as a graveyard," Cornford countered as he got to his feet and holstered his Remington.

"So let's bury them," the Virginian suggested. "Help to kill the time."

"You're pretty good at killin' things, ain't you, Steele?"

"We're two of a pair, like you said, feller."

The grin dropped away from the youthful features. "That guy in Friday Wells was the first I ever blasted. And these were all yours. One-armed man and a rifle—well, that's just one of the things I found out I couldn't handle so well after what Gorman done to me."

But he had done all right with the Winchester: resting the stock on top of his shoulder and working the action and trigger while the barrel teetered about with no support.

Steele nodded. "It never was us in competition. You just set them up and I knock them down."

"But you went for it, Steele. You've got both arms but somebody did somethin' bad to you one time. That account for those murders back east?"

"Let's get to work," Steele said, veering sharply away from the subject. "Before they start to rot in this heat and Gorman is warned off by their stink."

The grin came back, as bright as ever. "Maybe

145

I ought to stick with you and change my line of business," the kid said. "Become a mortician?"

"Keep drawing, feller," the Virginian drawled. "For a one-armed man, burying the dead is no easy undertaking."

Chapter Ten

The man seeking to avenge the death of his son came riding along the gully an hour after moonrise. Ed Gorman was a year away from sixty, but he had the build and strength and fitness of a much younger man. But his eyesight was not as good as it once had been. The gully floor was in deep moon shadow, but a blazing fire radiated plenty of light. He saw six horses tethered just beyond the mouth of the gully. And one man sitting up on the other side of the fire while five others lay under their blankets on this side.

"You've got 'em, Catton!" he yelled, his croaking voice betraying a mixed tone of anger and glee. He heeled his horse into a canter over the final few yards, swinging clear of the saddle and jumping to the ground before the horse reacted to the slack reins and skidded to a halt.

Steele watched from the cover of a humped pile of rocks beyond where the horses were tethered. He and Cornford had stacked the rocks, not primarily for cover but to make a crude grave for the dead men. More rocks had been moved to where the fire was lit, and these were covered with blankets to simulate the forms of sleeping men.

Ed Gorman did not realize the ruse until one of his running feet collided with a blanket-draped rock. He vented a cry of pain and fear, stopped dead and reached for his gun.

The shot with which Billy Cornford had killed Clifton Reese had not been a lucky one. He drew and fired on the rise and exploded a second bullet into Gorman before he was fully erect. And both were placed precisely where he wanted them.

With a roar of pain, Gorman spun into a half turn and sat down. Blood blossomed from two wounds in his upper right arm and the stains on his shirt sleeve merged. As Cornford stepped around the fire, Gorman tried to get out his gun with his left hand reaching across his body. Cornford fired the Remington twice more, not halting as he took aim. Gorman screamed as a matching pair of wounds were opened in his upper left arm.

Gorman fell backward to measure his length on the ground. In the firelight the lines of his quivering face expressed agony and pathetic confusion. A smile of evil delight was inscribed on the features of the one-armed youngster as he swung a leg to splay his feet, straddling the helpless older man.

"Name's Billy Cornford, Gorman," he said, and pumped a third bullet into his victim's right arm. It shattered the elbow. "You wouldn't remember it!" he shouted above Gorman's scream. The final shot from the Remington crashed into the left elbow.

"Please, no more!" Gorman begged. "It's the dude I come to get. Not you."

Calmly, Cornford stooped down and drew Gorman's Colt from the holster. "I bet you don't even recall the First National Bank in Springfield, Missouri."

The Colt exploded four times. Two bullets in Gorman's left forearm and two in his right. Pain had ceased to exist for the injured man. Shock numbed him and he sobbed.

"Kid who pushed a cracker barrel in your way and lost his arm on account of it. Now you're gonna lose both your arms, Gorman."

The Colt was emptied. One bullet smashing through the right wrist and the last doing the same to the left. Gorman's mind could accept no more punishment and closed down against the twitching nerve ends of his damaged body. He was plunged into unconsciousness, to gain a merciful period of release from the intense agony.

Cornford remained straddling his victim for long moments, then lifted a foot and swung clear. But he continued to stare down at Gorman until he heard the sounds of a horse moving. He looked around then, and saw Steele leading the gelding toward him, his easels, folding chair and supply of paper strapped to the saddle.

"On your way, kid," the Virginian told him. "You did what you had to."

"And you?" Cornford asked as he took the reins.

"I'll think of something."

Cornford's expression was incredulous for a

moment: not crediting that Steele would simply let him ride away. But then he gave one of his lopsided shrugs and sighed in resignation. He swung up into the saddle.

"I sure hope he lives," he said, eyeing Gorman. "I intended him to."

"He looks like a pretty tough feller," Steele said.

Gorman's breathing was shallow, but regular.

"I won't say goodbye, Steele," the kid muttered. "Because I'd sure like to meet you again someday."

"In hell will be soon enough for me," the Virginian growled.

"And that's sure enough where we'll end up," Cornford rasped, taking a final look down at Gorman. Then he wheeled his horse and heeled it into a dust-raising gallop—past the fire and along the gully.

Steele stood where he was until the thud of hoofbeats had faded out of earshot. Then he went hurriedly to work, aware that he had to finish before Gorman regained consciousness if his labors were to have any point.

First he removed some of the rocks from the grave and dragged clear the body of the man who most resembled his own build. Decomposition had already started and the Virginian had to fight the nausea back down his throat as he stripped the dead man of his clothes. Then he stripped himself naked and switched attire with the rotting body.

He dragged the body over to the fire and pushed its head into the flames. As the flesh bubbled and burst and gave off a sweet scent, the Virginian covered the grave and ran off all the horses except his own and that on which Gorman had arrived. When he dragged the body clear of the fire, its head was nothing but a sooty skull hung with fried chunks of flesh.

One final chore remained. From his saddlebag he took two pieces of stiff drawing paper and a length of charcoal: all stolen from Billy Cornford's supplies. One of the pieces of paper showed a drawing of the showdown with Phil Fish in the mountains. The title was long enough to enable Steele to do a fair imitation of Cornford's lettering on the blank paper.

THE DUDE WAS GOOD BUT BILLY CORNFORD WAS FASTER ON THE DRAW.

Steele pinned the paper to his own jacket now worn by the mutilated corpse, then mounted the gelding and rode him up the slope toward the gap between the mesa face and the tower of rock. Gorman was groaning back to agonized awareness as the gelding's hoofbeats faded into the distance.

It was important for Steele to stay out of sight until the word was spread and Billy Cornford met his inevitable end by a fast gun who didn't give a damn about the kid's missing arm. And the Virginian knew just the place he would go. He grinned quietly, relishing in anticipation the beautiful face and willing body of Rosabella Sierra.

"It wasn't an iron in the fire, feller," he rasped to himself. "Not exactly. But whatever, reckon my career as a gunfighter is . . . *over*."

THREE NEW WESTERN SERIES
FROM PINNACLE BOOKS

Read one—you'll want to read them all!

APACHE by William M. James

The savage saga of an heroic Indian, Cuchillo Oro ("The Golden Knife"), and his single-handed stand against the invading white man during the Indian Wars.

P306	THE FIRST DEATH #1	.95
P397	KNIFE IN THE NIGHT #2	.95
P525	DUEL TO THE DEATH #3	1.25
P692	THE DEATH TRAIN #4	1.25
P782	FORT TREACHERY #5	1.25
P827	SONORA SLAUGHTER #6	1.25
P913	BLOOD LINE #7	1.25

STEELE by George G. Gilman

Young Adam Steele begins a long bloody trail of revenge for his father's murder, carrying only his father's rifle. Inscribed on that rifle is the dedication that provides his inspiration: "To Benjamin P. Steele, With gratitude, Abraham Lincoln."

P558	REBELS & ASSASSINS DIE HARD #1	1.25
P713	THE BOUNTY HUNTER #2	1.25
P814	HELL'S JUNCTION #3	1.25
P846	VALLEY OF BLOOD #4	1.25
P871	GUN RUN	1.25

DAKOTA by Gilbert Ralston

Dakota has substituted Oriental martial arts and contemporary weapons for the bows and arrows his ancestors used, but this modern Indian warrior's battles in today's West are as crucial to the survival of his race as his great-grandfather's were.

P278	DAKOTA WARPATH #1	.95
P319	RED REVENGE #2	.95
P417	CAT TRAP #3	.95
P564	MURDER'S MONEY #4	1.25
P730	CHAIN REACTION #5	1.25

If you can't find any of these titles at your local bookstore, simply send us cover price, plus 25¢ each for handling and postage:
PINNACLE BOOKS, 275 Madison Avenue, New York, N.Y. 10016